PERLIE

JAY KASPERBAUER

Table of Contents

"I Could give a Damn About Some Horses"

A HORSE RACE CAN BE MANY THINGS, though it almost always falls short of fair. Onlookers are amused by the spectacle beginning with a unified ambling gait, clobbering a sand track. The horses' fury of rolling and shifting joints shimmer in the sunlight beneath their taut hide. Equine heads bob, their formations noble and expressions fixated. Some break away from the group, spreading out ahead and behind. Jockeys hover over the galloping beasts like pilots without jump seats, remaining mostly still in contrast to the stretching and rocking bodies of the horses propelled by the four-beat footfall. Horses thrust themselves forward while jockeys fight for the inside of the track. Sometimes riders in the lead remain close, other times they appear separated by track lengths.

Before the race, men are tasked with analyzing a cache of data and the racing secretary determines how many lead weights the horse will carry within the pads worn at its sides. These are handicapped horse races. The goal is to eliminate the chance of consistently wide margins so that the race at least *appears* tight. Thus, to some extent, the race becomes fixed.

But races aren't always close, and the man who bet that his horse would place had observed myriad outcomes at the horse track. In the past, he felt that he understood the outcome on the day of the race—as if he was tuned in intuitively. But after a couple of substantial losses, he was bucked from his winning stride. His confidence wavered and then he couldn't recover, but he still tried. Yes, he had seen losers win and winners lose. The bones of horses fractured and joints separated. Horses tumbled, plowing men head- and shoulder-first into a spray of sand, followed by a dust cloud that, when it cleared, revealed a pained horse and a lifeless rider. After an earlier race in which his horse placed, he saw the helmet of a jockey split in half like an apple. A horse race is an orchestrated rodeo for self-defined men of rank with money to lose. But in the case of the man that Uriella had come to observe, the money wasn't always his to lose. Return was hardly guaranteed, but the enthralling display of equine submission was certain.

The boorish returned to the track even after losing, yearning to feel their blood simmer again. The gate dropped down in the sand with a heavy thud and a thousand clomping hooves shot past the stands. Uriella saw the man begin to seat himself once the horses had passed. Around the turn, his horse, Parlor Trick, gained on the beast nearest him, and then overtook it. With his hand on the bleacher, the man froze in a half-seated stance. He immediately noticed the discrepancy in his compulsive routine. On all previous occasions, the race would start and he would sit, it was that simple.

In the beginning, when the money was his own, he was awed at how quickly it could disappear. Money he'd earned from contorting his body, grunting as he pulled, pushed, twisted, and wrenched, while sweating through a shirt slick with motor oil, could all be bet and lost in a moment. The handicapped horserace was rigged by definition—but that didn't stop anyone from betting on it.

The horses were already rounding the corner toward the side opposite him. Unsure what to do, fearing his break in his routine had already doomed him, and unsure what motion or positioning of his body would rectify the error, the man panicked and seated himself. People near him cheered, standing. Two horses moved past Parlor Trick on the straightaway. Then a third, too. Doomed.

In the box seats behind him, a sharply-dressed man with a calmer demeanor, named Arthur, walked through the crowd sure-footedly to fetch a drink for Uriella, the woman he had just met and was hoping to sleep with. She, aware of the effect she had on men at the racetrack, stood alone, watching the back of the large head of the seated man as he leaned in either direction anxiously, looking on at the track intently. The race wasn't looking encouraging for him.

The clean and proper man who craved the presence of Uriella returned eagerly with a clear plastic cup of champagne. He attempted to hand it to her, but her arms remained at her side.

"What are we celebrating?" Uriella asked before raising a hand to accept the drink. The man began to speak but ceased when she grabbed the glass and downed the champagne, deciding that it didn't matter. "Isn't it bad luck to buy it before the race ends?" she wondered aloud, enjoying the sweetness but detesting the way her teeth felt suddenly sticky.

"How about a hot dog, Art?" Uriella asked. It was an absurdly casual question asked in an intoxicating way. Blood now flooded his cheeks. "Don't they have those at the counter?" she wondered aloud, hoping to send him away again.

Arthur returned to the concession stand once more with his confidence slightly reduced. Again,

Uriella was left to her business, watching the anxious man seated several rows in front of her.

Uriella heard the scattered sounds of astonishment from the crowd and focused her attention on the track. Prince, one of the horses racing, had taken the lead unexpectedly. The man watching the horses remained seated. Arthur returned bemused, with a orangish frankfurter in a paper tray and a fist full of napkins. Ordinarily, she would not have bothered with such rubbish, but the evening's errands had left her with very little time to eat.

More cheering ensued and she took her first bite. Prince widened his lead and Parlor Trick continued to disappear into the back of the herd. The horses rocked and the jockeys bounced in a chaotic scene. At once, Prince dashed across the finish line, drawing an array of exclamations from the crowd, a few heavy howls followed by a collective murmur. Uriella finished eating and carefully blotted her lips with a napkin. The trash was handed off to Arthur domineeringly. His puzzled look reminded Uriella to play nice, so she smiled widely in an effort at reconciliation. The time had come for her to leave. After all, the race was finished and the man seated in front of her had obviously been defeated. Again.

After the race, the winners and impartial spectators who chose not to bet remained in the stands, gripping their beverages. The man whose distressed demeanor had been carefully observed stood and exited with the rest of the defeated.

Before Uriella's companion could even ask where she was going, she drifted into the crowd, following the man who had bet again on a losing horse. At the pavilion, she watched him fling his ticket into the trash. She saw him stuff his hands deep into the comfort of his trouser pockets, his bulky troubled head hanging low. Uriella removed the slip from the wastebasket as she watched the crowd engulf the conquered man at the exit gate. She looked down and read the filthy ticket.

Single Selection: To Place - Parlor Trick - Total Bet - $500

Uriella slipped the paper into her purse and carried on. As she made her way to her car, the man who was hoping for at least a kiss caught up to her, hollering, "Hey, wait! Did I say something? Do something? What, did your horse lose?" Uriella ducked into her esteemed coupe, the body of it unblemished glossy metal. She cranked down the window and her face emerged.

She took a deep breath, and then replied quickly, "I didn't even place a bet." She cranked the motor on. "I must be going. Thanks for everything, Art." Uriella zipped past the other cars in the lot and sped onto the freeway, leaving Arthur standing solitary in the parking lot.

On the edge of the community sat its abandoned oddities and outcasts. Industries that exist for pleasure or for profiting off one's vices are located some distance from residential areas and require travel to visit.

Uriella could see the heat shimmering from the city lights through the open passenger window. They looked like tiny eyes, twinkling from afar. Behind her was the casino and the track. Looking back from her silvery coupe she watched the back of the track bleachers, now a shrinking edifice that reflected the glowing orange of dusk.

She muttered to herself, "I could give a damn about some horses." Then, with one hand she pulled the knob to switch on the headlights, and with the other, she removed her bulky sunglasses. Meanwhile, her knee did the steering.

The coupe disappeared down the road toward the interstate with the windows down, introducing whiffs of dried sagebrush, hot pavement and arid desert. Later she smelled the sour decay of road-kill as she rolled along. The windows stayed down. Uriella had nearly arrived to report her findings to the financier at his office.

Up ahead, a wide canopy fanned fluorescent light onto a fuel station and travelers crossed in and out beneath. Next to the station sat a mini-golf attraction. It was a brief distraction for the children of weary drivers. The floodlights over the course were intense enough to compete with the light from the canopy next door. Uriella's approaching coupe held a different more acute energy that outshone the electric desert oasis in every way possible. It followed her everywhere, but few *really* saw it. Arthur might have missed it. But, the financier knew of it.

Ureilla's coupe came in fast then idled slowly when it reached the first fencepost of the minigolf course. With the car's windows down, the jazz saxophone on the radio reverberated softly—the primary marker of her presence now, aside from the car's low chugging motor. She killed the engine and stepped past the course and into the office of the financier.

The minigolf landscape demonstrated the outer fringe of oddities in its own maniacal way. The park sat flooded in light with its miniature freakish figures begging to retreat into darkness. There was a resting lion with a great mane and sharp teeth disproportionate to its gaping mouth. A strip of green carpet ran between the teeth and out through the back of his head. Tiny fairways flanked by painted boards were mitered perfectly, turning and twisting in unison. One hole sat at the center of an emerald island surrounded by stagnant water. A narrow gangplank stretched over the moat. Sitting tall beside one hole stood a miniature Ferris wheel. On one of the gondolas of the spinning wheel was a lifelike figurine of a frightened mother with her arms wrapped around her screaming children, each of her hands covering their eyes.

Tumbleweed rolled past a rule board carved with terse golf guidelines. Uriella's boss, the financier, could read them from where he sat inside the office, waiting. She entered and said, "He lost." Uriella set the losing track ticket on the desk and threw herself into a seat, crossing her legs.

"He lost," the financier repeated in feigned disbelief, still looking at the rule board outside the window. He mostly ignored the ticket, expecting no different really. Some part of him was mildly dismayed after all, even in the wake of repeated disappointment. It kept him sharp, his unwillingness for complacency in his dealings.

"You said it, when he first owed us. Didn't you?" he said to Uriella. The financier was reading one of the rules through the window. *Don't lean on the clubs.* Uriella shrugged. *Respect the course.* The financier didn't mind the language on the sign. He had someone write and post the rules when he took ownership of the roadside attraction as a result of what he considered someone else's bad debt. There was a modest stream of revenue and a quiet office for him to use.

When he began "dealing in intimidation," as he called it, those outside of his network knew him as "the Toaster." The nickname came about because it was said that, regardless of the situation, *he* determined the level of darkness. Those within his own circle didn't acknowledge the nickname. Others, especially the newer associates, never knew of it in the first place.

But Uriella was aware of the nickname, and the financier had known for some time that she knew. The financier and Uriella began working together in a sort of "partnership," as he called it. But he was the only one who referred to it in this manner. She went on with her illicit business as normal, quickly realizing the potential of their arrangement. But if her past desire for independence was any indicator, they both knew their partnership would eventually run its course. After which, she might be back when a situation called for it. The financier would let her, too. That's what he loved about her. If anyone could appreciate her radiance, it was him.

"Why does this high roller insist on losing all of his own money, so that he has to borrow—so that he can lose that too?" he asked inertly. Again, Uriella shrugged. The financier kept reading the sign. *Have fun and start golfing.* A period, no exclamation mark—his idea. Another tumbleweed rolled past.

"And we're the fools who let him owe," Uriella said, carefully picking dust from her lap.

The financier shifted his focus to the inside of the office, and then to her. "You'll visit him again, at work," he said, looking into her eyes.

"Of course."

"Maybe you can have an office like mine soon," he said. He was referring to the fiasco that led him to seize the minigolf business.

"I like mine," she said, tilting her head toward the coupe outside.

This made the financier grin unexpectedly. "We'll be in touch," he said and dismissed her.

"Good Luck With Everything"

PERLIE EXISTED, IF YOU COULD CALL IT that, within a fortified prison cell, self-contained and alone. Hardly anything moved in or out. The barrier was nearly impermeable. This truth weighed on his mind, burdening him more than the inability of his body to move beyond it. He felt that containment was the absence of his own free will.

He considered himself a man who had previously had a distaste for human interaction and conversation. His dislike for dialogue hadn't really been changed by his incarceration. There had been an energy within him when he first arrived that he wrestled a great deal with. Not so much a need to speak or even move, but an unrelenting desire to avoid atrophy, and to not remain static. He thought that inactivity in the company of time was really the same as moving backward. Everything and everyone outside his world moved forward, no matter what he was doing. Life kept going without him.

Stuck in a cell, he learned early on the value of distracting yourself. Within the concrete fortress, all he had was time, and he spent half of it inventing ways of getting the other half to pass. When allowed, he would read. Other times, he would replay a movie in his mind's eye, recalling it scene for scene as best as he could. Seldom did he reach the end before he grew bored, at which point he stared at the wall or fell asleep. Imagination can't make fools wise but it makes them happy.

It wasn't until nearly the end of his sentence that he found solace in physical exercise. He would complete pushups on the cold floor, sit-ups on the rigid mattress. Each time he pushed off the ground, he felt himself advancing with time, with the outside world. Movement propelled him and prevented him from reversing. The exercises were routine, especially in the mornings toward the end of his sentence. Pushups were what he found himself doing on the morning of his release, when the prison guard trotted down the corridor toward his cell whistling Reveille.

The sudden distraction made Perlie lose count of his pushups but he continued anyhow. When the guard got closer, he switched from whistling to imitating the sound of a trumpet—the honking heard each morning in the military. It went, *BERP BERP BERDER-DERP*. Perlie knew what it signaled.

The rest of the cell block had already cleared out by then, marching single file toward the commissary for breakfast. But Perlie didn't get breakfast the day that he was released.

The mouth trumpeting ceased and Perlie saw two shiny black boots touching at the heels, standing opposite the painted prison bars. He was on the ascent of a pushup and hesitated a moment before proceeding.

The guard asked, "You ready to go, or you want me to wait till you're done doin' pushups?"

Perlie stood abruptly, embarrassed by his pause. The gate unlatched and swung open and together he and the guard walked through the hallway, flanked with open cell doors exposing empty grey rooms. Perlie remained uncuffed— halfway to freedom, and feeling that way too. The guard reached into his chest pocket and pulled out a stick of gum and offered it to Perlie. Perlie obliged, relieved by the gesture. Together he and the guard savored the wintergreen gum. Perlie felt the flavor diluted by the eager flush of spit in his mouth, as he was reminded of the forgotten taste. Vigorously he chewed, splitting the gum in half with his teeth and kicking it around in his mouth with his tongue. Perlie felt his heart trying to eject itself from his chest onto the floor, anticipating the fleeting feeling of understanding that he felt with the guard, and knowing that he was about to face a room with several prison administration officials. Intimidating, Caucasian prison administration officials.

When he was younger, still adolescent, Perlie would have dreams about his father, Sylvester, whom he had never met. The spans of their lives had hardly intersected. Only at his birth did the timelines of Perlie and Sylvester briefly touch and then run off in opposite directions. Most of Perlie's childhood had been spent living alone with his mother—though mostly he just lived alone. His mother tried to earn an adequate living, not needing excess—a value that he shared later. She would often work well into the evening.

Syl had left the both of them when Perlie was too young to remember the details of the man's face, whose features bore a resemblance to his own. His mother would tell him that there was no possibility of him remembering what his father looked like, let alone could he dream about him precisely. She suggested that he could perhaps dream of his father *vaguely* and out of focus. Perlie's mother shared what few photographs of his father she had held onto—but those alone were insufficient to build the memories of him. It was only dreams that brought the adolescent closer to understanding who his father really was—more than the biased revisits by his mother.

And through those dreams—forced into his slumbering consciousness out of a desire for a patriarch, and adoration—Perlie began to recall false memories. Memories emerged more vividly from his incessant dreaming than from encounters that had actually occurred when he was a boy, arguably too young to remember. Memories of infancy were recalled obscurely in adulthood; early experiences were mistaken for dreams and truths became delusions. It was by this perplexity that for much of his life Perlie insisted that his father used to grab him by the shoulders and look into his eyes, saying, "Son, in life, you gotta grab the steer by the horns if you wanna take control of it." Perlie's mother scoffed when, as she was departing for work, he asked if his father ever used this phrase. But she went on out the door, never addressing the factuality of the phrase either way. So, imagined or not, this line stuck with Perlie throughout life. It didn't matter whether it had actually happened, because a recalled dream becomes a *real* memory.

Perlie saw the way his mother worked a full day, punching one time clock for hours only to pound another one somewhere else. She spoke of the necessity for hard work and only then would she willingly share positive recollections of his father. She told young Perlie about how his father was once more driven than her, working unending hours on the production floor as a sculptor. He brought home defective figurines and statues depicting religious figures—laden with cracks and notches from air bubbles and impurities—from the mill where he worked. Their tiny garden was scattered with unpainted effigies—uniformly dirty white, like tiny monuments of failure leaning askew in the bed of dirt. All this, Perlie's mother told him throughout his childhood.

Then Perlie's father took to different work—the kind performed under cover of darkness. Out of sight from lawful overwatch and out from underneath oppression, money was made in a way that he'd never seen before. Syl eventually lost his job when the yield of the illegal work beat that of the legitimate kind. Perlie's mother pleaded and begged, "If not for your own sake, then for the boy, so that he can grow up at least knowing his father." The law caught up to Syl frequently and honest employment become unattainable. Time and time again, he was tempted with the criminal sort of toil. That story, or what Perlie knew of it, was for another day. Though, it was one to be told no less.

Where the memories of Perlie began is difficult to say. After all, no one remembers being born. His life, like others, began in an instant, long before the dreams or memories took hold. The pace was abrupt from the start, like the unleashing of hell's horses on a track of fire.

When Perlie became an adolescent, he held fast to his father's lucid adage, and as a result began to encounter his own trouble. He was driven by a desire to control his own life by any means. This desire, coupled with the reckless abandon of his youth, led Perlie to few encounters with the law. They were facile, but so began a brief permanent record of his own—minor infractions committed to life like memories. He was thrust forward at an irreversible speed until the last crime, the most recent, occurred. That one had been punishable by incarceration at the state penitentiary.

"Don't be like your father, Perlie," his mother would often rebuke.

Perlie now exited from fourteen months of incarceration, served at a moment in his life when young men his age were supposed to be marrying mothers-to-be and assembling cribs in tiny new homes. These were all things that he wished for too but by way of another trajectory. He strived for the stability possessed by his peers, and for similar reasons. Perlie's desire was bolstered by his father's remembered—or dreamed—phrase, spoken to prove his ability to obtain all the things that his own early death prohibited. Syl's ambitions were fixed on crime and drowned by whisky. He drank until the bottle was empty—until it was dry, with nothing leftover to help him. Only in the final moment before his death was contrition recognized. Sylvester had one last realization of his inevitable demise when he careened over a curved road shoulder and burst through the side of a brick home.

Perlie wished now to redirect his own drive so that he might avoid that feared fate: plunging into incarceration or smashing through an occupied home in an automobile. Not cuffed nor killed—but if Perlie had to choose one or the other, he would have needed more than a few minutes to decide.

Now Perlie was a freed man who was drawn out of the nothingness that surrounded him, the mute grey penitentiary. He was outside, free again. His timeline and his life expanded as he walked forward, noticing the intense smell of blooming viburnum and lilac. The scent of damp grass was replaced by exhaust from passing motorists. His shoes were loosely tied and his eyes focused downward as he inhaled the swirling air. He felt gratitude for the familiar trill of robins in the trees above.

As he walked, Perlie reached down and pushed his belt pin through the rearmost hole of his leather belt; the opening that had remained unused until this moment. The pin finally gave way and Perlie pulled the end of the belt through the metal buckle at his waist. His pants were snugly-cinched at his hips. He lit a cigarette from a pack that he had left behind when he first arrived at the penitentiary. The tobacco was nearly petrified dust and tasted terrible. Maybe it was time to quit. Everything he carried with him now had been left behind at the check-in fourteen months ago, when he was less wise and a few belt-notches heavier.

Perlie was akin to a rough study of a stone statue, chiseled but not yet polished. His gut was mostly empty but his head was filled with the self-evident reflections of a cave monk. His sensitivity to temperature had become skewed during his time of hermetic cold—incessant unblanketed shivering in his cell now gave way to feelings of warmth in the spring breeze as he walked jacketless. Prison was *real* cold, he thought; a bitter cold originating in the surrounding concrete that passed into his body and seemed to coagulate his blood. He'd emerged a newly-capable insect, having shed his former self. He was prepared for breezy flight.

He felt a sudden frenzied rush—a thrill—and perhaps anger too. Perlie began to walk faster. An irrational thought entered his mind—what if the prison guards realized that there had been some kind of administrative error? He thought of them putting their hands on their holsters, hollering with rage: "*No!* That man—the one smacking that gum, he was *not* to have been released. *Quick*—stop him!"

Perlie pictured the vengeful eyes of the prison

warden—he envisioned him opening the gates and sounding the alarm as his little minions spread out like ants, weaponized and ready to attack; to strike out disorder. To break a man down and remind him that he had no home but a prison cell. Perlie's hair stood straight up as he imagined the warden's rigid voice yelling through a bullhorn, "Get your asses in gear and catch that man! He was *not* to have been released!"

Perlie shook off the premonition, but anger shot through his veins and his knuckles turned bloodless. His pace approached a full-fledged run, then. The distance between him and the penitentiary gates grew and Perlie felt the space expand in his quarried heart. He was running now, and he relished it—not having experienced the pace in the penitentiary nor felt it until this moment. He had grown accustomed to the slow trotting shuffle within the narrow hallways and prison yard. Perlie felt obnoxious and slowed a bit, feeling his heart beating rapidly. He saw his chest come out with each inhaling breath.

The morning sun cast a shadow beneath him, its edges lay at his peripherals. His dark outline was more defined beneath the single source of light—the sun—than it had been in the artificial lights within his cell. Perlie noticed the variations in perception—sight and distance and definition— as he moved along the road. He wondered how many days would pass before the novelty of this new perception was lost.

He enjoyed it all, the plain sounds otherwise taken for granted, now unimpeded by the vulgarities of convicts and shouting guards. No longer was he surrounded by the sounds of hands and fingers rattling along the chain link fence in the prison yard. Instead, there was the almost deafening silence of the natural landscape around him. The simultaneous rush of these nuances led Perlie to feel a sudden urge to shout—so he did, a short and raucous prison-yard expletive that cut through the chirping of the birds and rustling of the leaves. Perlie was embarrassed by the sudden outburst. Timidly, he approached the bus stop cutaway that sat beyond the far edge of the sprawling penitentiary compound. Another man who pretended not to hear Perlie's upheaval stood waiting for the bus, too.

Up pulled the penitentiary-commissioned bus, scooting close to the curb and stopping with a sharp hiss of air before opening its doors. The bus rumbled into town, carrying only the two men, each of them silently wondering from opposite sides of the aisle the fate of the other once they arrived downtown. Most released men met kin or arranged for transportation elsewhere, but Perlie had neither accommodation. His mother had since died, and there was no one with whom he shared blood residing within a hundred miles. So Perlie relied on arrangements by jail-coordinated housing.

The bus driver turned off from the highway, heading into town along a wide boulevard that cut through a peaceful neighborhood, eventually stopping at the courthouse to let the men off.

"Good luck with everything," the driver said bemused, pulling the doors shut quickly. Perlie felt dizzily sick as he watched the bus disappear behind the black smog of its exhaust. He stood still for a moment, waiting for the feeling of uneasiness to pass, hoping for the earth at his feet to cut him a break and cease rotation. He thought of how he might look wobbling to a bench nearby, how the conversation might go with a cop, how easily he might be accused of public intoxication, thrown back in jail.

He sat still—or as still as he could muster— and pictured his stomach, empty and constricted, shriveled and bound like an overhand knot. The urge to eat overcame him. Perlie reached into his back pocket and grabbed his wallet. He counted the bills. The contents were meager. The money could be stretched for a couple of days if he had to. Focusing on the bills held so closely gave him a sick feeling and he felt his chin quake with the sudden urge to vomit. He jumped up and darted toward an alley. Hunched over, leaning partially on an upended wood pallet, he voided a bright burning liquid onto the pavement. His throat was raw. His stomach was empty. With his sleeve, he wiped his mouth. A crow landed next to his vomit and waited for Perlie to leave. When he eventually walked away, the bird hobbled over to the mess and began to pick at it. On, Perlie trotted into the quiet afternoon, feeling desirably weightless.

In a bodega, Perlie reached beneath a heat lamp and grabbed the last deli sandwich on the counter. He pulled a cold glass bottle of soda from a cooler and paid for it all at the counter. When he was outside again, he unwrapped the sandwich and looked everything over. It was like he was a visitor in another country—now feeling this way even more so than before his incarceration. Before, the reluctant faces that passed him on the street, scrutinizing him coldly, had given him that feeling, as if he didn't belong. Now, the packages and labels of all the products had changed, too. It was all different than he remembered, some things were less recognizable than ever.

He wet his throat with the icy soda before biting into the sandwich. The cold pop nourished him and he gulped it down quickly. Soda was quite the privilege. This type of sudden endowment was rare if present at all in the penitentiary. The penitentiary, he thought. The last gulp of soda tasted sour—acrid from the thought of prison. Perlie vowed to never return. Going forward, his life would only include corrective action. He would avoid recidivism. He told himself that he could do it. He would avoid being stripped of the pleasures he had neglected all this time. He would avoid those vile but profitable deeds that were sometimes placed in his path.

Corrective action, the next most prudent, included securing the housing recommended to him, because not only was he a man who had served a prison sentence, and who had a criminal record—he was also a man who had been stripped of the cell that he had called home for the last fourteen months. No longer was he afforded a rigid mattress and paper blanket. Stripped bare, he resumed his life only with what he now carried.

"I Don't Like Bullshitters"

PERLIE CONSIDERED ANOTHER CONVICT AS true a friend as any, or at least as true a friend as was possible in the penitentiary—someone with whom he shared a mutual trust. His name was Sam, but like many other men behind bars, he was known only by his nickname: Deuce. *Deuce* was the identity that Sam took on.

The two of them were introduced early in Perlie's sentence. It was always with difficulty that Deuce recalled the exact duration of his own sentencing. It seemed as if he didn't really care how much time remained. Many inmates found this failure to recollect to be surprising, because, most of them could recite the exact time served, or the exact time remaining. Deuce was unlike most inmates. He had probably served at least a decade by the time Perlie was introduced to him. This was thought to be the case based on Deuce's under-standing of surviving life in the penitentiary—an understanding that could only be discovered by an inmate who accepted their predicament while time ticked on. An inmate chose either acquiescence or insanity, eventually. The ill-fated inmates fed hysterical disorder to new inmates, but Deuce carefully explained the role of each inmate to Perlie, telling him whose advice would be unsolicited and who kept to themselves.

While how much time remained on Deuce's prison sentence was never discussed between the two of them, the topic of Perlie's sentence duration was commonplace. And as Perlie's release drew near, Deuce mentioned to Perlie that he knew a man, a friend, who had provided jobs for released convicts in the past. The two men discussed the prospect briefly in the yard. On his second to last day in the penitentiary, Perlie exited a door into the open air and moved toward a group of inmates who spoke quietly and casually to each other. Deuce was seated beside them, ignoring them as he often did, as they all stood digging their heels into the dirt and nodding in agreement about something. Deuce sat alone but welcomed the company of Perlie.

"Perlie—hey, Perl," Deuce said and waved him over.

Perlie nodded and approached him. He remained standing.

"Your day … uh … is approachin', eh?" Deuce said.

Perlie propped one foot on the bench beside Deuce and nodded. "It is. And … it feels like that day, too … the day I might die. My day—*that* day." His voice sounded dry.

"Well, I don't mean *that*." Deuce shook his head and smiled. "And 'sides, you ain't dyin'. You gettin' out. That's livin'. That's life, man." Deuce paused and looked around the prison yard in envy, as if he was imagining the approaching feeling of freedom that Perlie was relishing. Deuce began speaking again before the jealousy took hold. "Know where you'll go? Or what you'll do?"

"Into the city … on the bus. At first, anyway. Can't imagine I'll go too far just yet." Perlie held out his empty hands. "Haven't got much to go on."

"Well, above all else, you know where *not* to go, don't you?" Deuce asked, still looking out at the yard. "*Not* back to … to a path that winds its way back in here." He pointed at the hard dirt below their feet. "Anywhere else is fine. You're a decent man." He stopped and smiled. "Or a decent man for a criminal, at least."

"Gee, thanks. Means a lot comin' from an ol' crook like you."

"But really. You ain't destined to return here.

29

Some men are. Some are trapped—even after they get out. Condemned. Can't ever get out. But not you. Makes me wanna do what I can to help you. You know? I always try to help anyone who stands a chance when I can. Anyone who shows promise of turning their life 'round outside a' here. The ones still young enough to do it." He sat up and looked at Perlie. "I think I may even have a job for you. A *real* job. Or at least I think I know someone who can help you some way."

Perlie always felt that he was an understudy of Deuce—someone to teach him all the lessons that came with a decade behind bars. They shared a desire to serve their sentence and reform—perhaps reflect—but nothing more. Deuce, though apparently unsure of his own remaining time, reluctantly (and just once, that Perlie could remember) explained that more time remained on his sentence than he wished to admit. So, perhaps it was his—Deuce's—recognition that Perlie was like him, but that he had more years of freedom ahead of him than behind him. Deuce wished to offer any help that he could, to aid in Perlie's reestablishment.

Perlie was pleased by the offer, but kept his composure. That calmness was shared by Deuce, who once told him, "A man who overreacts is a man who can't keep his own emotions in line. And, if a man can just up and erupt with emotion, how can anyone expect to trust him? Or respect him?"

Perlie responded to Deuce's offer now, quietly. "Thank you, Deuce ... really."

Deuce nodded. "The place, the job—it's at a garage. They might need a mechanic if you're lucky. Used to be on a street called South Oak. Mighta moved, I guess, but you'll find it. Anyway, the garage is called ..." He paused a moment and looked down. "*Auto*-something." He curled his lips inward and scratched his chin, finally saying, "Can't think of it now, Perl. Hell, it'll come to me. Hopefully 'fore you get out. Funny how quickly you forget somethin' in here ... in the absence of it. Memory degrades. Anyway, you'll remember *Auto*-something, at least? I know that much." Deuce powerfully tapped his fingers on his knees, like he was hoping to spark the connection of a synapse— still trying to recall the name of the garage.

"Yeah, I'll remember," Perlie said, and shook his head.

Deuce finally let go the failure to remember. He leaned over to Perlie. "Good. The man who I knew even 'fore our time in here is Freddie. And *that* I can't forget. Even in his absence." He laughed and looked out at the yard.

"Freddie," Perlie repeated. "I'll remember."

"He's a good man. Someone you can trust, at least. We haven't talked in years but I hear details from time to time as men come in and go out. And come back in again." Seated, Deuce

31

shifted his weight. His tone dropped an octave lower. "The way that messages pass among criminals—even in here—well." He waved his hand dismissively and then resumed. "A stand-up guy, Freddie. He'll understand your deal, your need for work. He's got a record himself—but he's straight now. Some men can do that. *You* can do that, Perl. Freddie—he does all right, from what I hear. And he ain't in here, at least. He's at that garage." He paused, hoping once more to recall the name. Still, he couldn't. He shrugged. "Worst case, he won't have a job for ya. But even then, I think he can at least point ya in the right direction. Freddie knows people. He'll be good help either way."

"I'll look him up right away," Perlie said.

"Good. And send him my regards."

During Perlie's exit briefing, a prison administrator suggested that he check out residency at an organization that aids in reintegration and housing. The desire by many penitentiary officials was to aid in avoiding recidivism for the released convict. In a home or out on the street, a free man wasn't the prison's burden any longer.

The organization Perlie had been referred to owned a modest complex that included four one-bedroom homes, all closely beside one another on a city block, but with enough space between them to allow for some feeling of independence.

Perlie decided that he had no choice but to pursue the arrangement, but he feared that life among other ex-convicts, including some who were destined to return to the penitentiary, might force him into trouble again. He feared the returning path that Deuce spoke of. Perlie had been a burden for the last year, relying on the penitentiary to provide meals, housing, reformation, and security. Like prison, a housing complex for individuals with criminal affinity might elicit new criminal scheming. One prison administrator told Perlie that it was the responsibility of the individual to uphold their own reformation. He couldn't forget that.

So he had taken their advice, and now here he was: trotting along the craggy sidewalk toward the city block where the halfway house sat. Perlie brushed his open palm along the neatly trimmed boxwood that skirted the walkway. A raised bed of blooming hyacinth sat just beyond it. The floral scent arrived at his nose and was then carried away by the breeze. Perlie kept walking beneath the shade of mature oak and maple trees, whose leaves shimmered in the wind like paper sequins.

Perlie approached the housing compound and saw the four quaint homes, whitewashed and gently weathered with broad convex roofs, like contemporary wigwams. In front of the structures, a ramp led to an office. Perlie could see through the window. Inside sat a woman at a wide industrial desk who appeared busy. Perlie marched up the ramp and when he got to the door, he reached out for the handle. The woman looked up, startled. Her concerned expression shifted into a kind welcome as Perlie entered. He returned a smile.

"Good morning," Perlie said. "I'm hoping to apply for housing. You have time for a walk-in?"

"Yes, yes," she responded, warmly. "Have a seat." Her skin was luminescent, and her dark coarse hair was wrapped neatly in a bun. Her stature was of tacit wisdom and power, her face tired skin. "Two a' the four units here will be available for occupancy, um ..." She paused and sighed. "Soon. Got my maintenance guy in there paintin' now. He should be finished some time tomorrow. He left a little early today." She looked up at the clock. "After all, it *is* Friday. Anyway, the good news is that I don't have any pending applicants at the moment. So I'll get somethin' ready for you quick as I can."

She turned her chair and reached into a metal file cabinet behind her, withdrawing a pastel envelope. She wet her fingers and grabbed an application from the top. Then, she laid the application before Perlie and turned it around for him to read.

"Please, please—have a seat and fill this out," she said. She pulled her glasses to the bridge of her nose and peered over them, looking at Perlie as he sat before her. "My name's Barbara." She smiled broadly. "Known 'round here as Barb. I pretty much live here, too, but in the event that I'm not around, I'm available by phone for maintenance issues, inquiries … complaints. My phone number and hours are on the door, should you need them. And, uh … I'm sorry, what's your name?"

"Perlie Quinn. Pleasure to meet you." Perlie shook the woman's hand from across the desk. Her gentle and accommodating manner made him feel the most relaxed he'd been all day.

"Pleasure, I'm sure, Perlie. I'm also here to aid in your integration. Or, your *re*integration, I guess I should say. Happy to advise any way I can. Employment, transportation, health and medical. Addiction services. Churches. Don't be afraid to ask." She was speaking to Perlie like schoolteachers and ministers had done when he was young. He felt like a child.

Barbara lifted her glasses and resumed working, signaling for him to begin. Perlie looked over the application briefly before touching his pen to the paper. Several minutes had passed as he worked through the forms. He avoided asking questions of Barb when he could, then laid down the pen carefully and she looked up, bringing her glasses down to the tip of her nose again.

"All done?"

"Yeah, yeah—I think so," Perlie replied. He slid the form over and she began to look it over.

"Where are you comin' from, Perlie?"

"From the state correctional penitentiary, ma'am."

"Here? Whistlewood?"

"Yes. Fourteen months, released today. Came straight here." He thought of himself vomiting in the alley earlier.

"And before that?"

"South Valley. Grew up there, with my mother."

"I see. No stranger here then, huh? She still living there? Your mother?"

"No," he said, warily. "She passed away while I was gone … during my sentence."

"Sorry to hear that." Barbara was looking over the application carefully. "You'll need to initial here, too." She rotated the page on the desk for Perlie. He signed quickly and slid it back to her. She resumed checking the forms over quickly until the last page. "All right, then. Everything looks ready to go here. I'll send this off for a background check and file the rest of it for you."

"Thank you," Perlie said, shifting in the chair.

"Now, most importantly: I need you to get back into society the *correct* way. Back to work and all that. You need help finding a job?"

"I hope not. I mean, I don't think so. I've been given the name of someone … at a garage."

"A garage?"

"Yes, *Auto*-something. I've got a little experience being a mechanic."

"How'd you find that so quickly? I thought you said you came straight here?"

"I did—someone I was close with in *there* … they knew of somebody who owns a garage. On South Oak, I'm told."

"Hm," said Barbara with some concern.

"If there's no job, I'll let you know," Perlie said, recognizing her skepticism.

"Good. I'd hate for you to miss your first rent payment. I'm forgiving—ask the others—as long as my tenants are doing everything they can to stay outta trouble. And remember, I'm here to help. If this *Auto*-job—you said *Auto*, right?"

"Yes, Auto … uh, he couldn't remember the name for sure, but the owner—his name's Freddie, I'm told."

"Right. If this *Auto* place doesn't pan out, you come back here right away and I'll see what I can help you find, 'kay?" She smiled in an uncertain but hopeful way.

"Absolutely. I will."

"Good. Now I don't like bullshitters. You're not a bullshitter, are you, Perlie? My ex-husband was. So were about a dozen others who sat right where you are."

"No, 'course not. I plan to start workin' right away. Promise."

"That's great. Our communication—it's imperative. Don't make me have to come lookin' for you—for any reason, okay? Other than that, I think we'll get along well. Don't you?"

"Yes, no doubt."

"Have you got anyone to stay with tonight, Perlie?"

"No."

"No?"

Perlie was already standing, ready to leave.

Barbara said, "Well, we keep a room open at the Sterling Motel. It's a little old place just off the highway. On Sage." She tore off a piece of paper and wrote down the address. "I'll call over there and let the folks know that you're on your way. Check in at the desk when you get there okay, Perlie?"

"Sure thing. Thanks again."

Perlie stepped outside and let the office door close slowly until he heard the latch click. A recollection quickly flooded his consciousness:

All inmates: outdoor time is OVER.

In his mind, he heard a loud buzzer playing over a loudspeaker. He pictured men complying, moving into formation.

Quietly form a line and return to your cells in single file. Quietly now. No funny business. Return to your cells.

The memory of the buzzing continued in his head. Then the mechanical click was almost audible—the sound of solid metal ejecting into its empty counterpart.

PLICK.

The door to Barb's office closed and he heard it again in his head.

Perlie paused outside the door. He was reminded that doors were accessible to him in either direction—his movement through the day would no longer exist only unidirectionally. No longer would he move through the penitentiary halls in only one way, listening for the *PLICK* of a locking gate latch behind him as he passed through each one.

"This Ain't No Charity"

ASIDE FROM HIS FRIENDSHIP WITH DEUCE, Perlie considered most other connections to be of little value in the penitentiary. Both he and Deuce avoided speaking with other inmates, especially those who were not to be trusted. They preferred instead to listen only and avoid conversation altogether. The discussions overheard by Perlie were mindless and unsubstantiated conversations about women and sex. On occasion, the other inmates would brag about their last lay before they were incarcerated. Other inmates listened in awe or tried to top the story with one of their own. But Perlie could tell when the stories were bullshit. An inmate could make any unfounded claim, creating their own stories and identities as they went along. When Perlie knew a story was true, it stuck with him. Either way, he could often feel the truth or falsehood bone-deep.

In his time in the penitentiary, Perlie noticed that old men often spoke truths. Their stories were rich with detail and each one held some unique significance to the inmates listening. One particular story that hung on tight throughout the remainder of Perlie's sentence and then beyond his release was told to him by an older inmate named Barney.

In the mess hall one day, as the inmates hovered over steel trays of steaming sludge, Barney told a story of a man serving a life sentence before Perlie arrived. This man had experienced cardiac shock that caused him to stop breathing momentarily. The coroner at the penitentiary legally pronounced the man dead where he lay inside his cell. But after several attempts at reviving him, the staff was able to resuscitate him, starting his heart again.

But the man should have died, and he took issue with his revival, for he had specified a do-not-resuscitate-order in the event of just such an occurrence. According to Barney, the man found a public defendant who agreed there was a case to be made. Together, the previously "dead" man and his lawyer took on the correctional facility by stating that the lawyer's client had already served his life sentence and had already died and therefore owed to absolutely no one an additional life sentence. The lawyer argued that he should have been released.

The other inmates, including Perlie, leaned in closely to listen to the story as it was told. According to the story, the man who was resuscitated wanted his lawyer to offer a plea for immediate execution if his release was nevertheless refused. Either freedom or death, he hoped for.

There was more from that story that impacted Perlie's sleep that night—the despair of the revived man who argued that he had fulfilled his life sentence spread deep within his mind. His actions were of desperate clemency. Barney told Perlie that this revived man was considered by any practical man to be very much *alive*. But the man who was resuscitated had been given an opportunity and he viewed the heart attack as his key for unlocking the fortified gate standing between him and his freedom. Barney said that an illusion like that can fall upon anyone while incarcerated. The illusion appeared in your life at precisely the right moment to deceive you most effectively. At the end of the story, the revived man was not granted his request for release. Instead, he was required to carry on with his sentence until it was finished. Only upon his natural death would his sentence be concluded. But for the recently resuscitated man, his argument was valid.

Perlie lay in his bunk later that evening after

Barney told the story, thinking about the manifestation of such an illusion. He wondered if he would recognize such a thing. He tossed in his bunk like a fish on land, his eyes fixed to the ceiling and then the wall and then the floor and eventually back where they started again. Perlie peered at identical flat planes of concrete, finding patterns and faces of people he knew in the imperfect cavities of the cement.

The day before his release, Perlie spoke to Deuce again. He asked how Deuce came to know and trust the owner of the garage, Freddie.

Deuce told Perlie that the two of them had known each other even before their overlapping sentences—from back when they were both still "innocent in the eyes of justice," as Deuce put it. He went on to describe how they had worked somewhere together on a railway yard. Deuce said that he and Freddie got along well when they first met. He smiled widely when he told the story. Deuce told Perlie about a time when he and Freddie had finished linking train cars together for a locomotive headed east for Chicago and then decided to take a quick lunch break inside a shaded railcar Freddie described to Deuce the idea that cosmic justice visits a person once and then goes back out of sight until it's entirely forgotten. Only at that precise moment does it come full circle with brutal speed, slamming back into someone's life like a loaded-down railcar.

That idea applied to revenge, too, Freddie apparently explained. One who gets vengeful with another person always finds themselves a victim to the same type of vengeance. No matter the cause of the vindication—whether it be love or crime or religion or getting screwed in a deal, plain and simple. Eventually, it would return. Apparently, both Freddie and Deuce felt that there was no means by which a person could predict the precise moment that the retaliation would happen. One could only guess when the rebalancing would occur. But as Freddie put it, you could always count on it occurring, "as sure as the sun come up." He even believed retaliation could appear on the day of a man's death, like an enemy seeking retribution. Incidents of revenge were witnessed throughout both of their lives. Deuce agreed—he thought men constantly found themselves to be victims of retribution only because they had acted with vengeance so frequently themselves. The reciprocating force comes back around again and again until a change is made—or, until death. Many times, that was the only way that lifelong behavior of incessant retribution would cease altogether. It wasn't easy for a person to make such a change.

Deuce told Perlie that he and Freddie would sit and discuss all kinds of things. Together they swore they could encourage world peace if everyone thought just like they did. If every man and woman knew the suffering that others had had to endure—people who immigrated to this country, refugees of another country's oppressive regime, poor people, those marginalized, and so on—if that *anguish* was shared by everyone in America, then *harmony* could be shared by everyone. A man who strives for harmony with conviction would rarely know such a troublesome revenge throughout life. The passive stayed out of the ring, Deuce explained. Everyone else, he said, took turns boxing inside the ropes, sparring and wondering why they were always getting punched by everybody else. When someone shows up in life with their fists clenched tight inside boxing gloves, you must decline going rounds with them. It's better to find a chair and sit out the fight. The universe—that *cosmic justice*—will sort things out, both Freddie and Deuce agreed.

Even with all the enlightened discussions on the railyard, the irony was that both Freddie and Deuce nevertheless ended up in the penitentiary. And now Deuce held Freddie in high regard for maintaining his freedom—for not returning. Deuce hoped for the same fate for Perlie—and not the irreversible destiny that Deuce had experienced. "Succumbing to revenge," as he put it.

In the days leading up to his release, Perlie's

conversations with old Deuce turned ceremonial, as if signaling the end of an apprenticeship. The few who sat in Perlie's place before him, under the leadership of Deuce, had mostly failed but he tried again with Perlie anyway. And now Perlie felt that he owed it to Deuce to uphold this idea that some good could come from spending time in the penitentiary—but only if incarceration did not recur. Incarceration had taught Perlie how to redirect his will to achieve and maintain freedom. He was his own captive now. The unrelenting power of will to achieve something was like holding a pistol to your own head, leaving yourself with no choice but to do the thing that will save you or else surrender to death. By returning to the penitentiary, you might as well be dead.

Perlie and Deuce's last conversation, which took place in the prison yard, was memorable for both. Perlie would never forget Deuce's stern face and subtle smile, nodding with real sentiment as he spoke. His glasses were narrow with round metal frames that outlined his eyes. Deuce shook his head approvingly, feeling that he had said and done all that he could. Deuce's nodding was a simple gesture of endorsement in an environment where widespread paranoia and overwatch were commonplace. Perlie remembered that final expression that Deuce wore before the guards called them all back in—his face tilted up slightly and hushed like a monument.

Perlie's conversations with Deuce were all in the past, now. Onward, Perlie trotted as a free man toward the highway and the Sterling Motel as the sun lowered in the sky.

His legs began to ache, and he felt like he was on an unending path that was leading nowhere but was prompting vivid recollections. Time spanned before him as his life was carried forward. Perlie was beginning to wonder if he was going in the right direction so he quickly ducked into a filling station to confirm the location of the motel.

A clerk with metal-framed glasses stood erect behind the counter. His squint was obnoxious and suggested confusion. Befuddled, he glanced at the door as Perlie entered. The clerk exclaimed, "Hid-ey-ho there, young man."

Perlie said hurriedly, "Can you tell me how much further the highway is?"

"The highway!" His head and torso rotated stiffly on the same axis as he looked out the window. He paused and thought deeply, finally saying, "Not too much further, buddy. Probably another mile. You'll see a sign for it soon, reckon." The clerk looked from the window at Perlie now with the same curious squinting look he had when Perlie entered. His nose was twisted back and his cheeks lifted his glasses just barely off of his face. "Where ya headed?"

"Sterling Motel," Perlie said, and looked down at the scrap of paper Barb had given him.

"Sure! The Sterling Motel. Not too much further once you get to the highway, buddy. Just off Sage."

"All right, then. Thanks." Perlie waved.

"You got it, buddy," the clerk said. He drummed his fingers on the filling station counter, still squinting obnoxiously. Perlie walked back outside.

Down the road, Perlie caught a glimpse of the motel sign lifted high above the roofline. Shadows grew long and the space between buildings started to grow dark as the sun lowered in the sky. Fluorescent signs flashed on and flickered all around him. Traffic flowed past as he approached the motel on foot.

Perlie stepped inside the office and stood at the reservation desk. The door was propped open by a broken block of asphalt from the parking lot and the inside smelled of damp carpet and dirt. Scattered on the window ledge were plants—dying or already dead. Dried and browned ferns with shriveled petals sat in a layer of dust. The smell was exacerbated by the low sunlight flooding the dusty window case. Behind the counter was a man carefully postured, standing but leaning on a tilted stool. The man looked as though he might topple from his careful pose. He was preoccupied with a hangnail but his eyes eventually averted, looking up at Perlie briefly. Then he resumed with the nail. "Hello. How can I help you?"

"Checkin' in for the night," Perlie replied. The front desk manager could probably have guessed where Perlie came from just by looking at him, but he let Perlie tell him anyway. "I was sent here by Barb ... uh, Barbara. From the halfway house."

The manager reached for a clipboard and a pen and handed them both to Perlie. "You'll need to register like the rest of 'em. Fill this out then I'll get you your key."

The front desk manager lifted himself from the stool and it rocked until it was steady again on the ground. The man was short and his bottom jaw protruded like a bulldog. His lips recessed where teeth were missing. Perlie recognized the manager's arrogant smirk, his disdain for delinquent ex-convicts.

"I'll have to send someone up to the room, it ain't been cleaned yet today," the manager said. Perlie acknowledged him with a nod, his head still facing down as he wrote. He finished the form and handed it back across the counter to the man. "If you don't mind a mess you can still get set up in there. Long's you don't mind." The manager spoke condescendingly. Perlie played his part cordially, like he had done with others before—carefully smiling and asking politely. The manager disappeared behind a partition and came back with a key. He extended his hand lazily, loathing the offering.

"Here," he said to Perlie. Unable to help himself, he spoke again quickly—with the inflection that Perlie recognized. "And we don't put up with no funny business here from all you. This ain't no charity. We ain't but a stone's toss from the police station. I got no problem calling the cops if I need to, understand?"

"You won't have any problems from me, mister," Perlie replied, leaning more toward a sarcastic tone than he knew was productive. He was tired and wanted to be left to rest. "I'm not homesick for jail just yet."

The front desk manager studied Perlie for a moment. He conceded with a grunt and hopped back up on the stool, going to work again on his thumbnail.

Perlie headed for the stairs hung from the edge of the motel outside the row of doors. He looked down at the plastic key tag and found his room.

When he entered, he was pleased to find that the bed had been made. Doubting that anyone was actually cleaning the room regularly, Perlie was glad that the room looked as though the last guest had left it in order. Perlie decided to do the same thing upon his own departure from the motel.

Beneath his back, the bedsprings creaked when he laid down. Sunlight fanned out from the gap beneath the door. Perlie sat upright again and looked for a phonebook. Finding nothing, he called the front desk manager.

"Damned thieves," the manager said over the phone. "The last guest must've taken it." Perlie was looking carefully at the Bible that sat inside the end table instead of a phonebook. He placed it back in the drawer and pushed it shut.

"You don't happen to have a phone book down at the desk that I can borrow, do you?" Perlie asked, regretting his earlier mocking tone and hoping it wouldn't prevent this one last favor.

"Yeah, I do," the manager replied. "But you better come down here to use it. I'm not lettin' this one walk off too."

Perlie set the phone down and made his way to the front desk. The manager reminded him, "You gotta use the phone book here."

Perlie reached for the phone book but before the manager let him take it he looked up, out the window, noticing the door to Perlie's room. "Hey," he said. "You didn't shut your door."

Perlie turned, saw the open door, and said, "Oh, I'll be quick. Shouldn't matter much, anyhow—I didn't bring anything here with me worth taking."

The manager's eyes widened and he raised his eyebrows, saying, "Maybe nothing of *yours* worth taking, but that room is furnished after all, ain't it?"

Perlie realized his mistake and said, "You're right. Won't happen again."

"In a place like this, leaving a door cocked

open like that is just an invitation for criminal activity," the manager said.

"Understood—I'll make this quick," Perlie said carefully, and opened the phone book to the business listings. Beneath the bold heading, "automotive," several listings were bulleted. Only one of which started with *Auto-*. Perlie remembered Deuce's words.

Funny how quickly you forget something in here. In the absence of it.

The phone number listed was for a garage called *Autopia*, on South Oak. That had to be the one—Freddie's garage. "Can I borrow your phone quick, please?" Perlie politely asked.

It became apparent that the front manager considered Perlie to have some nerve, that the favors and handouts didn't seem to end with him. The manager lifted the receiver and base with both hands like a newborn and set it carefully on the desk before Perlie.

"Thank you." Perlie recognized that he'd likely have few chances for more favors.

He dialed the number for Autopia. The line rang on, unanswered by anyone. There was no answering machine, either. Perlie hung up the phone but kept his hand gripped on it firmly. He picked it up and dialed the number again. Again, no answer. Perlie looked at the clock and considered the time while the line rang. Discouraged, he thought he'd better wait and try again in the morning. He hung the receiver back on the base and slid it back to the front desk manager with care.

As Perlie turned, the motel line trilled loudly from the front desk. The manager quickly answered. "Hell-o, Ster-ling Hotel." Perlie paused and waited.

The manager spoke into the phone. "Uh-huh. Nope, not me. Where you calling from?" Then he looked up at Perlie and asked, "You tryin' to call Awe-tope-ya?"

Perlie jumped back to the desk and took the phone from the manager and held it to his ear. "Yes?" he said, stretching the corkscrew cord as he stepped away from the counter. "This is Perlie."

The voice on the other end asked, "Yeah, man. You try callin' here just now? What can I help ya with?"

"I'm looking for Freddie," Perlie said.

"This is him. Who's this? You work at the motel or something?"

"What? No, sorry. That was someone else."

"Well, hell—what's his problem? Sounds like he's got a mop handle lodged up ..." Freddie trailed off.

Perlie looked at the manager and smiled, saying, "A stool, actually." Freddie let out a hearty laugh from his gut through the phone. The desk manager's tolerance was dwindling but Perlie cared less the longer he spoke to Freddie.

"That so?" Freddie asked. "Well, Perlie, what can I help ya with?"

"I'm … lookin' for a job. At your garage, hopefully. That is, if you're hiring." Perlie felt like he was fumbling a bit. He cut to the point. "A friend of mine—of both of ours actually—told me to call you. Deuce is his name."

Perlie paused, hoping that he wouldn't have to mention the penitentiary or his sentence in front of the manager, who he thought would likely take great pleasure in the shameful admission.

"Deuce!" Freddie said, excitedly. "Ha ha! Ah! Deuce. Shee-it. So—you met him? Still in the pen then, I take it? Makes sense why you at that run-down hotel, then. I suppose if Deuce got out, too, he woulda at least tried to call me." Freddie paused, thinking. "But, yes. *Hell* yes—I need a mechanic here, as it turns out. They don't seem to wanna stick around very long anymore. What you know about cars, Perlie? Anything at all?" He didn't let Perlie answer. "Either way, you can learn. I can teach you. Hell, I taught 'em all. I'm lookin' for someone dependable more'n anything, really."

Perlie replied, "Good, good. Well, I do know *some* … at least a start. I've worked on cars before, a little. But I am willing to learn." The front desk clerk rolled his eyes.

"Shee-it. Good 'nuff, then," Freddie said. "Listen, I'm 'bout to head out for the night. Was just walkin' out when the phone rang. If I don't leave now I'll be here all night, man. And I gotta be back early tomorrow anyhow." Perlie heard Freddie fumbling around on the other end of the line, his voice cutting out. "I gotta meet someone across town tonight ... so I gotta go." Freddie paused, apparently looking at the time, then speaking again. "Shee-it. I'm late. Say, Perlie, can you meet me here tomorrow mornin'?"

"Of course. What time?"

"Uh, I open up the shop, usually ..." Freddie paused again, as if he hadn't yet decided what time he'd start his day. "Eight in the mornin'? No—wait, I got someone comin' to meet me here. Bullshit *never* ends. Come in after. I should be done 'round nine a.m. We'll start then. I can show you round the shop. Can you be here at nine?"

"Yeah, of course. I'll be there at nine."

"Terrific. See you tomorrow mornin' then. Uh ... say, real quick, then I gotta go—Deuce holdin' up alright?"

"Yeah, yeah. Under the circumstances."

"Good ... *under the circumstances*. I like that. Well, rest easy tonight. I know the feelin' of just gettin' out. Get to bed early, and sleep if you can."

"I will. Thank you, Freddie. See ya tomorrow."

The other end of the telephone line shuffled briefly and then cut out. Perlie handed the phone back to the manager.

"Congratulations," the manager said sarcastically.

Perlie stood beneath the scalding spray of a shower, after vigorously scrubbing the penitentiary filth from himself. He stood beneath the flow of water in a daze while his skin brightened and his internal temperature began to feel feverish. When he exited the shower, his skin was raw and new—wiped clean of the bits of microscopic grime that settled into the gaps of his fingers and toes like tiny passengers smuggled through the fortified penitentiary gate.

Perlie switched on the motel television and spread himself widely on the bed. On the public access channel was a big-time pastor from Las Vegas who was being interviewed about a new chapel that had undergone a major expansion in congregation and capacity. The hard-nosed pastor expressed himself sternly and appeared a worthy man of God, spreading His message all over television. Speaking to the community of viewers, the pastor said that "*All* should consider finding God, and if you already have a relationship with Him, then you should certainly strengthen that relationship through the church."

The pastor spoke with pity as Perlie barely watched on, sunken into the motel bed, his eyelids slowly shutting. The pastor argued that the newly remodeled chapel was "worthy of consideration by anyone seeking God."

Perlie drifted like an empty boat half on shore and half in the water. The television pastor went on: "You shouldn't wait any longer, *no*! You must find God now while you are of able mind and body. Through God, all remain strong—even at their most vulnerable and when the days are darkest." Perlie's eyes were closed now in the dimly lit motel room. The television pastor continued: "Those who wait to seek out God at the eleventh hour will surely perish godless, moments before the hand strikes the hour."

Perlie sank into a deep relaxed state that almost went beyond common sleep. He dreamed of the time a bright and cheery young girl named Anna Sue caught his attention in school—a time in Perlie's life when others might have already considered him hell-bound. Young Anna Sue wore bright red ribbons that contrasted dramatically with her pale skin. Draped across her virginal neck swung a crucifix made of fake silver, attached to a chain by a tiny hoop. She had said that it was a gift from her father from when he visited Rome. The family of Anna Sue gathered at the First Episcopalian each Sunday for church. Beforehand, her eldest brother attended Sunday school with her and afterwards they would join their parents in the chapel. Perlie dreamed on, suddenly finding himself dressed in his best clothes, attending Sunday school as an attempt to position himself closer to Anna Sue, who he admired—no, obsessed over. It was the idea of association that was luring. But suddenly and reluctantly, he found himself closer to God. A divine light shone from God onto Anna Sue and her shimmering crucifix-bearing chain. Perlie, a godless boy, stood beyond, in her shadow. Her older brother noticed Perlie's ploy, his false faith, and called him on his bluff, in front of the entire congregation. In the dream, the television pastor learned of it too. How silly when a disguise was revealed for what it is.

Perlie's memory-mingled dream was halted by a sudden attention to the television pastor, who was still speaking. He was still asleep on the motel bed now. "If some kind of judgment day, day of reckoning, were to happen today and all men and women across this great land were subject to it, those choosing to deny God and live sinfully having their souls stripped from their bodies and of this earth, who would remain? Would *you* be among the holy who remained? We must ask—"

Suddenly Perlie was jolted awake. He switched off the television and the pastor's face froze mid-speech, appearing horrified with his mouth agape and then the image flattened and shrank to the center of the black convex screen before disappearing entirely, like a newspaper being sucked out of a speeding car window. Perlie climbed beneath the bed sheet and shut his eyes again.

The following morning in the motel room, Perlie put on his only shirt and tucked it into the loose-fitting pants in the faint light. He ran a comb through his hair in the mirror and took a look at the coarse stubble on his face. Curiously, he pulled open a drawer beneath the sink and found a plastic razor with a few bits of hair in the not-yet-rusted blades. He shaved and rinsed his face.

Leaving the bathroom, he wondered about the ex-convict who had occupied the motel room before him, sleeping in the bed. What, if anything, had actually been cleaned in this room before his stay? Perlie hoped to spend this evening in the bed at the halfway house—a clean bed, all his own.

He pushed the door open into the morning air and heard birds calling, sounds of traffic, and motors humming. He felt the warm sun drape over his body as he pulled the door shut, hearing the *PLICK* again. But this time, he thought, *I'm halfway to the halfway house.*

"Don't Wind Up Back In Jail"

IN THE WARM LIGHT OF MORNING, PERLIE marched from the motel over broken pavement lots—barren and empty save blowing trash and busted bits of glass. Corrugated semi-trailers were bordered by concrete dividers and oxidized chain-link fences. A lone tennis shoe was mounted upside-down on a broken fence pole. Entire blocks were surrounded by mute concrete with windows sparse. The industrious background made Perlie remember his last job before incarceration—at Sunland Produce, a wholesale distributor of fresh fruit. Nearly a dozen refrigerated box trucks were responsible for delivering goods to restaurants all over. Depending on the day, the drivers covered a great deal of ground—stopping off at restaurants like Mama's Bar-B-Q, Benny's Fine Chinese Cuisine, or Sal's Steak Joint. Their drivers, including

Perlie, started hours before dawn, when the kitchens had finally cooled off from the bustling evening before.

Perlie had been inside many restaurants, either on his own route or when he was filling in for absent drivers. Some of the other drivers were often unreliable but no one thought that *he* was unreliable. But on the subject of pay, Perlie and his boss Dennis could not reach an agreement. Perlie had asked for raises on more than one occasion, but Dennis would act too busy to discuss it. After Perlie insisted again, his boss, Dennis got angry, saying "Get a second job if you're so concerned about how much money you take in each week. How *you* spend your money isn't any of my concern. Why do *we* always gotta make up for *you* not knowing how to save any money?" Dennis said it just like that. He ignored Perlie's request and instead spoke vaguely about what he perceived to be the real problem with handouts and pay in America. Never mind his preference for employing drivers who he felt he could trust, ones that *made their own way* and *looked* like him.

One morning, Perlie woke for work at Sunland nearly fifteen minutes late. Knowing of his already strained relationship with his boss, he threw himself out the door twice as quick as he usually did, and drove that fast too.

When he got to the warehouse, Dennis hadn't

even noticed Perlie's tardiness, thankfully. Perlie was lucky, because Dennis had been waiting for just such a punishable offense—one he could point to the next time Perlie asked for a raise. Perlie was relieved that Dennis didn't see him come in late but the incident didn't go entirely without consequence. A cop on a motorcycle picked Perlie up as he crested the overpass doing sixty, and stuck him with a ticket after harassing him about the ownership of the car he was driving. Perlie told the officer that he was late for work—but to the cop, this was just another excuse. In disbelief, he smiled impishly, and told Perlie that he doubted he even had a job, and that he was going to write him a ticket anyway. The cop said, "So, the next time one-a *you* needs to run to the liquor store in a hurry before it closes, you better think twice." The cop said it just like that—just like Dennis did. Just like every heavy-handed person did when they felt the need to remind Perlie of his subservience.

The job at Sunland Produce was still Perlie's to keep, but the inability to pay the speeding ticket posed a problem. He thought about calling and begging—pleading to extend the due date until he could pull together some money to pay the fine. Instead, he came clean with Dennis, hoping that he might advance Perlie's paycheck in order to keep him on the road. But eventually he lost his license for failing to pay the ticket.

Dennis kept Perlie around, unlicensed, in the warehouse depot, cleaning and maintaining the delivery trucks. He had been told by Dennis that the old man who had been in the position before him finally retired. There was talk among the crew that the old man had been forced out to save money.

Just like before, the other drivers occasionally called in sick or asked for a day off here and there. Perlie waited anxiously for such an event so that he might see who his boss would rely on to cover the shift then. He didn't imagine that he, without a license now, he would be asked to drive. Some nerve Dennis had, after seeing Perlie ride the bus to work each morning until he had saved enough to pay back the fine. Perlie didn't feel that he had a choice and needed the job, so he agreed to it. So Dennis continued to use Perlie, underpaid and unlicensed, to fill shifts as if there was nothing even to consider. Meanwhile Dennis devised a plan. If Perlie were picked up driving one of his vans without a license, Dennis would play dumb and point to the fact that it must have only been recently that Perlie had his license revoked. Perlie would unknowingly corroborate this. Dennis would blame Perlie for failing to notify his employer of the suspension, and then Dennis could finally fire him. And in the interim, Dennis began to search for a replacement for Perlie. But for the time being, both men would take what they could get from each other.

It was on a Friday when a different plan began to take shape instead—one that unfolded quickly. One that eventually reached Perlie. A friend of Perlie's named Chambers, who was a cook at Riva's Taco, devised a plan that he thought would be beneficial for both of them. Chambers knew of Perlie's troubled relationship with his boss, and he himself, too a person of color, had undergone a lifetime of unfairness by oppressive supervisors in the workplace, until he finally found a job in a kitchen owned by a charitable Latino man. Still, he hustled on the side when an opportunity arose.

At the stop at Riva's, where Chambers cooked, Perlie would generally pause for a cigarette and a quick chat after he unloaded produce. It became a Friday routine, much like the call-off of the driver who was supposed to complete the route that day, but rarely did.

Together, Chambers and Perlie stood beside a stack of milk crates, with their backs to the wall. Chambers wore an apron reeking of sautéed spices. He took the matchbook from Perlie once he was done lighting his own cigarette.

"You still fillin' in for that slacker-ass cracker, I see," Chambers said and inhaled quickly.

Perlie scoffed. "Ha. I pretty much count on it about once a month nowadays."

"Yeah, well. You always fillin' in. For everybody, sounds like. Seems to me it would solve a whole bunch of people's problems if your boss ... what's his name?"

"Dennis."

"Yeah, Dennis—if your boss, Den-*ASS*, just loaned you the money so you could get your license back. Then he could just give you this route, you know?" Chambers had a clear goal in sympathizing with Perlie, but Perlie didn't mind.

"Tell me about it. He won't do it though—I've asked," said Perlie.

"So, what you gonna do?"

"Work somewhere else," Perlie said, then looked at the end of his cigarette as he inhaled.

"Yeah, that's one idea. Go work for somebody who gives a hardworking man a chance to prove himself."

"I hear you, man." Perlie wanted to change the subject, and to avoid the indignation that he was beginning to feel. It was late in the afternoon on a Friday, right before Perlie would have to return to the depot and face Dennis. "How are things going here?" Perlie asked.

"Good. Real good. But you know ..." Chambers lowered his voice. "It don't always add up. That's why I keep some business on the side."

"Yeah, with that cousin, right?" asked Perlie.

Chambers nodded his head in an exaggerated

way. "Don't know how long it's gonna last. My cousin acts more paranoid every day."

"Oh yeah? About what? Gettin' busted?" Perlie asked, glad the topic of his boss was behind them.

Chambers nodded again and said, "He thinks word got out about the thing—how the operation goes, you know—the delivery. That's when he's most vulnerable—when somebody's out deliverin' for him. And lately that's been *me*."

"So what? Quit before you get busted, man. You don't want to give this up." Perlie nodded his head toward the restaurant.

"It ain't even *that* that's got me worried. It's the freedom—if you can call it that. I'd rather be held down out here than in shackles, you know? But I don't think it's like that. I don't know what he's so uptight about. Think he's on the stuff, too. I never see anythin' when I'm 'bout to deliver for him. Always got my eyes open and my head on a swivel, actin' cool but aware, you know?"

"Yeah, I bet." Perlie said. "You gotta."

"But, now it's *him* that's got me worried. My cousin. So paranoid. So, I don't wanna take any chances for a while." Chambers took a deep drag of the cigarette. "Gotta deliver tonight for him but I'm thinkin' … 'bout backin' out. Who knows, though? Lord knows I need the money."

Perlie smirked and nodded. He didn't know what to say. He was more worried about paying off his fine than he was about exposing himself to the kind of trouble he'd encountered before.

Both men quietly finished their cigarettes. Finally, Perlie flicked his to the ground and stomped it out. He turned and saluted Chambers.

"I better be getting back or he'll be on my ass soon's I walk in the door," Perlie said. Chambers sent him off and Perlie climbed into the cab of the box truck. He pressed his foot on the brake pedal to start it. The tail lights lit up and the engine fired. Chambers acted coy, like an idea suddenly came to him even though he had been scheming since Perlie arrived. He jumped over to the truck and slapped the back of it, hollering to Perlie. "Perlie, wait up!"

Before Chambers even reached the cab window of the box truck, Perlie knew what he was going to ask. He rolled down the window with Chambers standing there, waiting to talk, deciding if he would let himself be involved.

Now, having finally reached the garage after the trek from the motel, Perlie noticed a two-door coupe parked neatly at the curb. He wondered if it belonged to Freddie. It was cloaked in a different kind of grey—shiny and metallic against the mute gray backdrop. The hubcap coverings were polished perfectly. On either side, the sparkling vision was bordered by rusted-out work trucks. A short garage sat tucked in among the industrial buildings, with a façade of patched mortar—cracked and repaired. Then cracked again. Pushed off to one edge of the front stood a door entirely of glass. Centered in it hung an illuminated *open* sign. Opposite the door, occupying more than two thirds of the frontage, was a large overhead garage door, cocked open rigidly, like an eyelid. A truck with worn out green paint sat along a wall outside. Perlie learned later that it belonged to Freddie. Hand-painted and faded with time, a low arch of shadowed block letters spelled *Autopia* on the glass.

A woman wearing a bright dress abruptly exited through the glass door, pulling her heavy sunglasses down over her eyes. Walking hurriedly, she didn't notice Perlie, and ducked into the silver coupe on the street. Perlie heard the ignition and then the sound of crushed sandy grit under the pressure of the wheels on the asphalt. The coupe sped away with a disappearing low mechanized hum. Perlie paused, still noticing the smell of exhaust.

Perlie was sold out by Chambers. Betrayed, so that Chambers could get a better deal for himself. A drug force detective had been on the tail of Chamber's cousin for weeks, surveilling his distribution network carefully. On the evening the police moved in, a box truck painted with colorful vegetables on the side was seen leaving the house where Chamber's cousin manufactured the stuff. Police hustled in on the big produce van, finding it full of uncrated boxes stuffed with drugs wrapped in opaque film.

Chambers was alone in the truck. Perlie wasn't even there. After he was arrested, Chambers maintained his story, but after some time a detective caught him in a lie, and Chambers confessed to having an inside man at Sunland who let him use the truck. At first, he tried to keep Perlie from getting into trouble—suggesting that Chambers used their friendship to gain information about the security of the trucks from Perlie unknowingly. But then the detective exaggerated their ability to convict Chambers and profited off his fear. They squeezed him until the names were all wrung out, one by one. Everyone in his cousin's operation went down. Then they focused on Perlie and Sunland Produce. The cops even questioned Perlie's boss, Dennis. But it didn't take more than thirty seconds for the detective to realize that Dennis detested Perlie—speaking kindly of his reliability but otherwise using the interrogation to lecture on the apparent laziness of "those people." Dennis told the detective that Perlie was unlike the "hard-working men, like you and I, who founded this country and fight hard to keep it from going all to hell."

Conspiracy to commit a drug offense—that was the charge. Perhaps there was truth in Perlie's story, that he really was ineffectual in the scheme. The police found it inconvenient to believe that a man with past convictions did not truly know better.

The exhaust from the silver coupe was carried away with the breeze, and Perlie advanced over the curb closer to the garage. He stepped in through the open overhead door after briefly deliberating. Inside the double garage bay, the floor was swept clean, but remained cracked and discolored—worn differently across the surface.

On the walls hung shelves of boxes with their facing panels half cut out for quick access. The boxes hung neatly near the tops of the walls at the ceiling. Below, pegboards were mounted where space allowed. Gaskets, hoses, lines, and fittings were organized by size. Organized clutter was the theme, and a thin overlay of dust and speckled oil covered most everything. The air was crowded with the smell of petroleum and lubricant. A faint sound of hissing air and whirring fan motors echoed inside the bay. On the wall hung a radio, wired snugly and suspended with flattened tinfoil over the antenna.

"Hey! You must be that jerk from the Sterling Motel with the stool lodged up his ass!"

It was Freddie, joking and laughing as he entered the garage bay from a doorway that accessed the front office space. Perlie shook his hand firmly, appreciating his wide smile as he came closer. Freddie's face was as large as a ham. His eyes were cool and kind. Coarse black hair speckled with strands of grey was cut short atop Freddie's massive head, and his face and features appeared wisely worn. Freddie pointed up to a convex mirror fixed to the corner opposite the doorway and said, "I saw ya walkin' in. I'm Freddie, by the way. You Perlie, I take it?"

"Yeah, you bet—sorry about that," Perlie replied, pointing to the open garage door. "I wasn't sure which door to come in through." He looked around carefully. "Anyway, really nice shop you got here. One of the neatest I've ever been in."

"Good! So, you *have* been in a garage before, at least. That's more than I can say about my last guy."

"A little, here and there," Perlie replied. "Uh, before … you know. But none like this." He continued examining in awe and went on. "Looks like you got everything you need in here."

"Well, hopefully. That's the point, anyhow. Like to get stuff fixed quick, ya know? Don't like messin' round waitin' for parts to arrive. For me, too much clutter's dangerous. Now come on—I'll show you round, Perl. Can I call you Perl?"

The two of them discussed in detail where parts could be found, with Freddie pointing to places in the garage bay where general categories of parts were stored. Perlie was shown a large metal tool chest with deep drawers filled with wrenches, sockets, and drivers—tools of cast pot metal were worn with time but organized neatly by size. They glimmered beneath the fluorescent shop lights like tone bars on a glockenspiel. Freddie spoke of his shop with great pride as he showed his newest mechanic around. Perlie followed him into the front reception area, where Freddie explained he could often be found. There, or in his office at the rear of the hallway. "If you ever need anything, just shout," Freddie said.

Perlie explained what knowledge he had of engine maintenance and repair from his last job. Then they moved back to the garage bay and Freddie demonstrated how to complete job orders and time sheets to track labor for each repair. He explained that he used the labor slips to write invoices for charging customers—something that he insisted on doing himself.

Freddie explained, "I like to keep an honest shop. People know when you're screwin' 'em. I don't bother foolin' round with my customers— overchargin' 'em, and all that. They catch on eventually and then they just take their business somewhere else."

Perlie nodded. Freddie went on. "And, I'll try and always be honest with *you* too, okay? I expect the same. Some things, neither one of us wanna know about the other. My past, your past—we here now, so let's focus on that, all right? Here and now and the *truth*. All liars are criminals, but not all criminals gotta go on bein' liars. And that goes for ex-criminals too."

"I can do that, no problem," Perlie said. He was beginning to let his guard down, like he had done with the lonely old inmate, Deuce. Something he had hardly done with anyone else. Perlie began to wonder about how he might get a message to Deuce—thanking him for setting him up at the garage.

"Good," said Freddie.

Perlie was overjoyed, knowing he was free and employed. He agreed and added, "What else does a man with nothing but the shirt on his back have but his words and the truth—right?"

Freddie laughed. "Shee-it. You *definitely* spent some time with that ol' sonofabitch Deuce."

For the remainder of the day the two men spoke casually as Perlie watched Freddie do the repairs that needed finishing. He would point out different things to Perlie—ways of approaching a repair and troubleshooting and so forth. Briefly he spoke of the mechanics who preceded Perlie. Freddie spoke defeatedly as he explained that the last mechanic had left some time ago, leaving him as the sole mechanic in the garage.

Freddie was bewildered by his inability to keep a mechanic in the garage after providing them income and a near guarantee for ongoing work. He explained that past mechanics sometimes ended up falling in the trap of crime again. That was how he described it, too—as a trap. Some mechanics were back behind bars. That was one of the risks of employing ex-convicts, Freddie explained.

There were stories of successes, too. Years ago, Freddie employed a man who worked at the garage for over three years and then decided that he wanted to open his own garage. So Freddie helped him get set up. To this day they remained friends. But Freddie hated to see any of his past mechanics leave for any reason, and he said he would always know when the time had come and a mechanic was done for good—for whatever reason. Freddie explained the feeling—he'd wait for them to show up for work one morning as the minutes passed slowly. After a while he could just sense it— the utter quietness of the shop and the phone as Freddie waited, perking up like a dog each time a car passed by on the street, hoping they'd show up.

"Back behind bars or in a grave—makes me sad. And *mad*. But if somebody quits for a better job or more money—whatever, I'm happy. Rarely, a mechanic will leave for a beautiful woman—and you know what? That can be forgiven. You can't blame a man for upendin' his life for a good woman. Seems to me a man'll do almost anything under the direction of the right woman." Freddie laughed.

When Perlie returned to the Sterling Motel he arrived at his room to find a handwritten message stuck to the door saying to call the front desk. He called down to the manager and was told that Barb had called from the halfway house and wanted a call back right away. Again Perlie found himself borrowing the phone at the front desk. Over the phone, Barb told him that he could check out at the motel and meet her back at her office.

"Good news, Mr. Perlie," Barb said over the phone. "We're getting you in here tonight! I can get you a bus pass starting tomorrow. But, I'm afraid you'll have to hoof back to my office today. How long do you think it'll take you to walk back here, anyway? I really need to pick up my girl. I got it—how about I leave the key to your unit beneath the doormat, outside the door? It's the one on the southwest corner of the property."

Perlie recognized the gesture, potentially a test to gauge the degree to which he could be trusted. He was glad for the act, never mind the reason—so he agreed.

"Great," Barb said. "I don't generally like to do this, Perlie—I do apologize. I left you a packet and some pamphlets inside your door. But do be sure and stop at my office tomorrow to go over the rules, okay? And Perlie—did you find a job? At that garage?"

"Sure did—the one I told you about," he said.

"Oh that's great news. Think you'll get along just fine here. I gotta run but I'll see you tomorrow, okay?" He agreed and said goodbye and hung up quickly.

The manager, perched on his stool again, said, "So sad to see you go so soon." He smirked, and Perlie pretended not to hear him as he walked out. "Don't wind up back in jail," the desk manager said, but Perlie was already outside on the sidewalk.

After a long walk, Perlie arrived at the sprawling halfway house precisely at the hour when the slow humming of lawnmowers ceased and people were gathering around their tables for dinner and ice cold lemonade.

Across the yard between the homes, the shadows of tree branches stretched in the low summer sunlight. A tenant sat on a plastic chair outside another unit on the property. He gave a subtle wave when he saw Perlie approaching. Perlie waved back and then bent down and retrieved the key from beneath the rug outside his door, the unit that Barb had described over the phone. The mechanism only gave way a fraction of an inch when he inserted the key, but not enough to disengage the deadbolt. So he turned the key in the opposite direction—or attempted to, only to find that it didn't move at all that direction. Perlie went back the other way again, jiggling the key while turning. Eventually, the deadbolt gave way. The lock apparently required a precise amount of force and proper key placement before granting access—as if it was teaching Perlie a confidential handshake that he would have to replicate each time he needed to enter.

With the other hand he turned the doorknob and swung the door open inward. The space was void but the air remained warm from the intense afternoon sun. Perlie turned on the first light switch he found and began to open the windows, letting in a faint breeze that made the blinds dance. Their pull strings clacked like plastic wind chimes. He moved around the small space, turning on switches and opening every door he could find.

In the empty cabinets he found stagnant air that smelled of solvents and fresh paint. The bedroom door would swing partially open all on its own if it wasn't latched, leaning with the foundation. Window cases and corners of trim were off square, each to their own varying degree. It felt a bit like a carnival funhouse.

The unit was furnished with only a bed and dresser, and some sheets and towels. From the bathroom door, a mirror hung, its surface streaked by a cleaning rag. Perlie made his way back to the entry room, adjacent to the empty kitchen. He leaned against the counter for a moment, feeling large when compared to the quaintness all around him. Sure, each room by itself was probably just barely larger than the penitentiary cell he used to call home, but after all a tiny jail cell was intended to compress him. This space had the energy to broaden.

Before going to bed, he stood in the shower again, with his eyes absently gazing at the edge of the tub, as the water hit his back.

Don't be like him, Perlie.

He wondered how his father felt when he was first released. What had he been thinking? He wished he could ask him. Perlie planned for a different trajectory. He wouldn't miss out on freedom again, like his father had. The two of them, so far as Perlie could tell, were cast from the same mold.

Don't be—

Perlie tried to picture his face again. Sometimes, recalling it would take much concentration. Now he had it, or at least a composite of it—his father's face, drawn up from the photos. There was a cigarette hanging from his mouth and his huge grin looked all too familiar—not like one from his father, but like one he'd seen somewhere else, more recently.

Then he knew it—that smile belonged to Freddie.

"Just Stick With the Oil Change"

"WELL. BACK FOR ANOTHER DAY?" said Freddie, eagerly.

He unlocked the front door and held it open so Perlie could walk in first. Perlie had been waiting a few minutes for Freddie to arrive, sipping coffee from a foam cup with his shoulder against the cracked stucco. Freddie turned the lights on inside and then said, "Hope you weren't waitin' too long. See you got coffee already." Freddie reached the switch beneath the neon *OPEN* sign and toggled it over. "I'm runnin' a lil' bit late this morning," he added. "Was out a lil' later than I like to be, but hey—I had to celebrate, ya know? Now that I got a new mechanic to help take some of the burden."

"Wasn't waitin' long at all, Freddie," Perlie said.

"Casino never closes," Freddie said. "Guess there's a reason for that. Ain't no downtime in that business." Perlie followed him into the garage bay and Freddie showed him how to turn on the overhead lights and air compressor. Then he asked Perlie to pull the first car around into the bay and when it was parked just right, Freddie had him operate the hoist to lift it in the air.

"I want you to know somethin', Perlie. Some of the people that come in through that door, they ain't too kind to us. Some of the people that enter that door still treat me like I'm in my prison blues, ya know?"

"I believe it," Perlie said. "They were treating me like that *before* I went in in the first place. But, what can ya do? You can't help how they act. Like that damned man from the hotel."

"That's true. What can anybody do? I'll tell you what I'd *like* to do." Freddie lifted a wrench in the air. "But I guess you gotta take the high road when you can. These people—some a them—they wanna see you lose your cool and mess up again. Nothin' would give them greater pleasure than seein' you gone, back in prison."

"They'd never admit it," Perlie agreed.

Freddie shook his head no disappointedly. "Well, I 'spose we better take a look at what we dealin' with here. Sound like an alternator issue." They stepped beneath the lifted car and looked up.

"Freddie," Perlie said. "Thank you for the job.

Really. And if you got some way to let Deuce know, I gotta thank him too."

"Don't mention it, Perl. Maybe someday. But let's hope it ain't either a us that get to tell Deuce the message in person. Say, let's turn on that stereo." He pointed to it. "You like jazz, Perl? What you listen to?"

Perlie ducked beneath the elevated wheel and crossed over to the wall where the stereo hung. The antenna looked like a child's science project.

"And turn it up some, would you?" Freddie asked, cranking a wrench. "Gotta drown out the poundin' in my head from all that pilsner." Freddie laughed again and Perlie turned the volume knob. Improvised piano keys rang out and a cymbal tapped along steadily. "Hey, there you go," Freddie said in a sleek and even tone.

The work went into the early afternoon, with Freddie pointing out what he was doing as he moved along. After explaining what to do, he would let Perlie take the lead, sometimes leaving him alone so that Freddie could answer the phone or help a customer. Together they began to feel comfortable with the new dynamic in the shop. Freddie mentioned that he couldn't believe the speed with which they could troubleshoot and complete repairs now. It had been awhile since the garage was that productive, he said.

The morning moved quickly, fueled by jazz arrangements on the radio. Finally, Freddie asked, "You hungry? How 'bout I grab us some subs quick? Lunch is on me today—after that you on your own." He grinned, wiping his hands on a rag, using it to clear the sweat from his forehead. "Stay here," he said. "I'll be right back. Just answer the phone if it rings, will ya?"

"Sure thing," replied Perlie.

He kept busy while Freddie was out getting lunch, not even thinking how long he'd been gone. Freddie returned quickly. Perlie heard him whistle as he came in through the door of the garage. He set the sandwiches wrapped in parchment paper on the front counter and continued whistling like a songbird as he drifted through the hallway. He seemed to be whistling the same melody, over and over. There was a quick staccato buildup—a progression, followed by several long drawn out notes that fluttered at the end. Then the melody went back high again and started all over. Freddie hung onto the low note for a while before starting it over. Each time he repeated it, Perlie found himself identifying what part he thought would come next.

Freddie stuck his head through the door to the garage, leaning in and holding himself from falling forward with his hands gripping the doorframe. He was still whistling. Then he stopped and asked, "You ready to eat some lunch?"

They moved to the front waiting area, where they sat and ate. Two rows of plastic molded chairs were fixed on either wall in the corner. Jazz echoed softly from the garage radio. Perlie heard the quick succession of raps on the snare during a drum solo but he couldn't make out any of the other instruments from where he was sitting. "You getting used to this station yet, man?" Freddie said between bites.

Perlie shrugged indifferently and said, "It's not so bad. Keeps you moving."

"Sure does. What do you listen to, Perl?"

Perlie paused after chewing and said, "I grew up listenin' to some blues, a little country western. Whatever my mom had on the radio, I guess."

"Damn. Country. Sorry to hear that." Freddie tried to keep a straight face as he began chewing again.

"Ain't so bad," Perlie said and smiled.

"Hell, man. Guess I can't argue a man's taste in music. Depends on the mood, I say. I like to give everything a try least once you know? *All* genres, at least once. Might not dig 'em, but otherwise how else you gonna know what you like?"

"Sure. I get you."

"I had this guy here, workin' for me once. He didn't like the jazz station." He pointed in the direction of the radio. "Always puttin' it down. Even when they played the greats—Count Basie,

Bird, Miles Davis. He'd tell me it was all rubbish. Maybe he was tryin' to get under my skin, I dunno. But I said to him 'This is music, man! Jazz won't be forgotten. Not never.' And I told him, 'You think it's rubbish? And the stuff you listen to ain't? What's that say about your taste, man?' And you know what he tried tellin' me? What his argument was? He said, 'Man, I think people don't even really like jazz music.'"

Freddie took a bite, then went on mocking the mechanic, saying, "He said 'People don't even think jazz is any good. They just say it is and pretend to like it—trying to convince everybody else. But really they just tryin' to convince *themselves* that it's good.'"

Perlie shook his head and laughed. He took a bite of his sandwich, still shaking his head in disbelief. Freddie went on. "We got along, me and him. But that damned man was always tryin' to get my motor hot." Freddie took another bite and chewed before speaking again. "I don't mind if you don't like it, is all I'm saying. I can learn to get along with just about anybody."

Freddie smashed his wrapper into a ball and threw it in the wastebasket as if it was a basketball. Perlie finished eating shortly after that, and they stood up in unison.

Freddie began to feel more comfortable leaving his

new mechanic alone in the garage bay while he focused on paperwork in his office. He kept busy with customers at the counter, handling business on the phone, too. In between tasks, Freddie would sometimes lean into the garage and check on Perlie. The check-ins throughout the day could be brief. But other times it seemed as though Perlie couldn't get Freddie to leave him alone long enough to get back to work. He thought Freddie was probably just glad to have someone to talk to in the garage again.

That afternoon, Freddie was sitting casually, looking over a trade magazine while Perlie investigated a suspension issue beneath a hoisted vehicle. Freddie stood and leaned his head into the garage with his hands braced against either side of the door frame. "Gonna use the bathroom quick, man," he told Perlie. Before he turned, he asked, "Is it the coils? They wore out?" Freddie figured it could wait and walked toward the latrine at the back of the hall with the trade magazine under his arm. Perlie resumed working beneath the car silently. He forgot to keep an eye on the counter while Freddie was in the back. Sometimes it was difficult to hear the door open from inside the noisy garage, especially over the radio. Suddenly Perlie happened to look out through the doorway, and saw a man standing at the counter.

"Hello!" Perlie shouted, setting his tools down

and rushing toward the reception area. "Hello," he said again, stepping behind the counter. "What can I do for you, sir?"

The man barely looked at Perlie. Instead, he appeared to examine the shop critically. His face was pale even in the shadow beneath his billed hat. He sported an unshaven chin. His eyes conveyed restraint as he continued to look about. He spoke emotionless. "Do you have time for an oil and filter change?" he asked and turned his head. Perlie noticed his Roman hawk-nose, the prominent bridge, and his heavy square jaw.

"Uh—think so," Perlie said, and looked at the clock on the wall. "I can squeeze you in. Come back at six and I'll have it done." Perlie glanced out the window at the lot and noticed the car. "Is it that one there?"

The man turned slowly and said, "Yeah, that's it. Belongs to my mother. Told her I'd take care of it for her today. But say—there's a chance I won't be back until first thing in the morning to pick it up. What time do you open, just in case?" He spoke with the same bothered inflection he had entered the shop with.

"I'm here no later than eight in the morning," Perlie responded. "But I could leave the keys in it when I finish it up tonight, if you'd prefer. If it's easier I mean."

"No, no. Absolutely not. I don't like that—can't

trust …" The man looked down at his wristwatch and thought briefly. "I usually take it to Simon Brothers but my mother failed to make an appointment this time. Now I'm dealing with it. I've never been here before … you'll take care of it? I can trust that you all …" He looked around hesitantly. "I can trust that you all do things by the book here?"

"Yeah, of course," Perlie said. "We'll take care of you."

"Good," the man said, perhaps unconvinced. "Just stick with the oil change. I'll be unavailable this afternoon, so if you find anything else the matter with her car you can tell me when I come to pick it up. Then I'll just have my regular shop take a look if that's the case. For now, just focus on the oil and changing the filter, okay?"

There was that look that Perlie knew well. That commanding tone, too.

"Sure, I got you," Perlie said sharply.

The man reached for the keys and set them on the table, but before he removed his hand from them he looked at Perlie sternly and said, "I know about this place, okay? About you all." He made a sweeping gesture with his free hand. His face was solemn, the aquiline nose aimed forward at Perlie. Perlie could feel his hot pulse throughout his body suddenly. Neither of them said anything. Suddenly, they both heard the toilet flush from the back of the hallway. The man removed his hand from the keys on the counter and exited through the front. Just then a police cruiser crept casually into the lot and the man climbed into the passenger seat before it hurried onto the street.

Perlie tried to relax, standing still when Freddie approached him from the hallway behind. "You all right?" he asked, and looked at the keys. "Somebody came in while I was on the john, huh?"

"Yeah," Perlie said, turning back to the garage bay. He didn't want Freddie to see him inflamed. Before stepping through the door threshold, he said, "A cop." Then he proceeded through.

"Huh? A cop? That don't look like no cop car to me, Perl." Freddie looked out the window.

Muffled, from beneath the hoisted car Perlie said, "It's not. That's his mother's."

"Well. He's a good little boy then." Freddie was paging through the magazine again, seated behind the counter. Perlie didn't hear Freddie but continued to work anyway, still trying to bring down the pace of his heartbeat. "Don't worry 'bout that guy," Freddie said, at the same casual volume.

"What?" Perlie hollered from the garage.

"I said: Don't worry 'bout him!" Freddie shouted.

"I won't," Perlie muttered to himself, quietly.

The large overhead garage door was open all the way for most of the afternoon. Perlie had left it that way when he pulled in the car belonging to the cop's mother. He'd finished replacing the filter and flushing the oil, careful not to spill any of it on the engine. He was inspecting his work carefully when Freddie walked in abruptly and said, "Hey man, you all right?"

"Yeah," Perlie responded, hunched low over the top of the open engine compartment. He carefully wiped away any blemish he saw. "Why?"

"You in your own head, man. Got all quiet on me." Freddie stood next to Perlie.

"Yeah. I'm all done here, just making sure everything's buttoned up," Perlie responded. He carefully lowered the hood and latched it, wiping his fingerprints from the glossy hood.

"Good. You don't wanna have to go back to the pen on account of forgetting to put the oil cap back on some pig's Olds, do you?" Freddie chuckled. "Everybody knows that's ten years in the clink. If you're lucky." He hit Perlie on the shoulder in a friendly way. Perlie flinched and smiled.

"Relax, man. Just tryin' to get your motor hot. Just a joke, all right? My bad, my bad."

Perlie replied, "Yeah, yeah—I know. I'm good, Freddie, promise."

"You *need* a drink. You drink, right? Come on, let's go over to the Piñon Pub. You ever been?" Perlie entered the car and Freddie approached the garage door opener. "You play pool? Come on, a pitcher of pilsner and a game a pool. It ain't gonna kill ya, Perl."

"Yeah, all right," Perlie agreed. He got in the Oldsmobile and backed slowly out of the garage and into the lot. Freddie began to shut the garage door. The car glided out into the sunshine in the lot, the overhead door closing just behind it without a moment to spare. Perlie trusted Freddie—the way he carried himself when he had reason to be agitated, like Deuce. Freddie switched off the lights in the bay and locked the doors. He and Perlie climbed into Freddie's old work truck and backed out onto the street.

At the Piñon Pub, Freddie ordered a pitcher of pilsner and two frosted glasses. He asked for a quarter for the billiards table, too. Then he sailed over to Perlie and handed him one of the glasses and poured it full while he held it in his hand.

"Thanks," Perlie said.

"Certainly, my man," Freddie replied.

The light was dim inside but was intermittently washed with bright sunlight when the door swung open as working men filed in to catch a quick buzz before heading home. Perlie looked around at the place, thinking humorously, *This is what I have to look forward to now*. Freddie held up his glass, so, Perlie raised his too. "Cheers," he said.

They each took a long drink. Perlie inserted the coin and began to rack the pool balls.

"Listen, Perl," Freddie said. "I appreciate that I can count on you to open up the garage in the morning. And to watch the joint while I'm on the can and whatnot."

"Thank *you* for the job, Freddie," Perlie said.

"'Course. It's been nice these last couple days, since you started. Ain't always been like that. Things'll get easier for both of us, all right? You just gotta hold on, keep pluggin' away. We'll get there." He looked around as a group of men entered, wearing chalky work boots and canvas coveralls. "The workin' man—that's you, now, Perl. They's some honor in that, trust me. And it sure as hell's better than being an inmate. Though sometimes I wonder ..." Freddie paused and looked at his beer closely, briefly thinking. "No, no, 'course not. Only kiddin'. Both situations got they grind. Day-to-day stresses and whatnot. But I'd rather be free and miserable than locked up and miserable. Wouldn't you?" Freddie laughed and took a drink.

"No doubt. I agree with you there, Freddie. You wanna break?" Perlie asked.

"You break, kid," Freddie replied. Perlie slammed the cue into the pool ball and the rest of them scattered across the felt table.

"Stripes," Perlie said, after knocking one in. He began to set up for his next shot. The voices of the other men grew inside the bar. Men laughed heartily and intermittently glass cups clanked and thumped on the tables.

Freddie said, "It's great, ain't it? These my people. Your people. All kinds of people. Good, modest ones. Humble, and all that."

"Yeah, I hear that. Nice little place—never been before," Perlie responded, setting up his third shot now. Freddie emptied beer from the glass into his throat and picked up the pitcher to refill it. Some beer spilled onto the floor as he poured.

"Yeah, I like it here," Freddie said. "Don't get hung up on that cop, all right Perl? He ain't nothin'. No big deal. You gonna find that all kinds of people like that enter that garage door. Sometimes I swear they come in just to ruffle my feathers. They know my history. Yours too, prob'ly. But they still come in 'cause we're quick and we're cheap. And most of all, we don't play their game. Nothin' but nice, even to the cops. And the rich snobs, too." Perlie set up another shot. "Shee-it, you gonna let me play or what?" Freddie asked and laughed.

"You seein' this?" Perlie asked, regarding his technique, the score. Freddie's mind began to wonder. He was thinking deeply—not about billiards but about the garage and money. He was starting to feel the pilsner go to his head in the hot evening air of the tavern.

"See, Perl, in the world, some people got more

than they need. And some people, well … they *need* more than they got." Freddie wiped the foam from his mouth with the back of his hand. Perlie took another shot but scratched. He'd heard Deuce say this phrase before, inside the penitentiary. So Perlie quickly finished the phrase and said, "Just a matter of gettin' us all together, isn't it?"

Freddie grinned wide as Perlie handed him the pool cue. "I taught him that," Freddie said and took his first shot at the table.

"I Think He's Dead"

THROUGHOUT HIS LIFE, JUDE BLYTHE rarely passed an opportunity to selfishly advance himself or his career. All situations and outcomes were considered swiftly and meticulously as he grew older. When he approached young adulthood, pressure mounted to make a name for himself in his chosen career, law enforcement.

Going back to his childhood, he first encountered such an opportunity for advancement, one that led him to take a bicycle at the ripe age of eight years old, so that he could more quickly finish his paper route and thus pursue a second route, which paid a dollar fifty more. The bike was taken from the side of a garage, and belonged to a neighborhood boy who often picked on Blythe for his appearance— his geometric face and his high-arched Roman nose.

"What'd you do, Jude?" he'd ask. "Catch your nose on the edge of the kitchen counter?"

When the bully wasn't making jokes, he was bragging about his bike, which he cared for greatly, but often failed to bring inside at night—leaving the perfect opportunity for a young Blythe to take it for himself.

The next summer, young Blythe had stretched several inches taller, and so he decided to take a job as a farmhand. That paid better than the paper route but required more strenuous work. He thought of it as a real character-building job. No longer needing the stolen bicycle, he sold it to a rural kid for what he would have paid for it new, had he paid anything at all for it to begin with. The result was pure unequivocal profit. He held on tight to the money he made from the sale of the bike and after getting paid by the farmer at the end of the summer, Blythe had enough to buy a car. Each move he made was carefully calculated with the goal of personal progress—like a child crossing a creek hopping from one stone to the next.

After graduating high school, he decided on a career in law enforcement—a decision aided by an uncle on his mother's side, who was a veteran policeman himself, and who recognized an ability for persuasive authority in his young nephew. This ability was possessed by lawyers and politicians too, but generally was distinctly authoritarian when expressed by cops. Blythe was persuaded, and succeeded early in his career. His eagerness to work and to learn was quickly recognized by the senior detectives. His inability to decline an opportunity for advancement brought him to the increasingly frequent midnight busts sponsored by a chief detective. Blythe would never turn down the late-night calls for action, though they were usually thrown together with little warning. There's always work for a man who will see that it gets done, day or night, when every other person is busy resting.

Now, he looked his face over in the mirror and sneered, running a cheap plastic comb through his thin hair. He looked at his square jaw and aquiline nose and thought of when he stole the bike from the neighborhood bully.

It was almost midnight and Blythe had been asked to meet the chief detective responsible for the operation, Officer Bledsoe, in a quarter of an hour. He had to travel several miles quickly after receiving the phone call from Bledsoe, who had provided the address for the rendezvous. Then Blythe would arrive routinely, meeting the other cops and detectives for a quick briefing before rushing the scene. Busts happened in homes and apartments where minor criminal enterprises oper-ated. Usually mostly empty, the places contained a few furnishings and personal belongings sitting among plastic baggies and scales, and shrink-wrapped powders packed like bricks. These things were sometimes intermingled with weapons and cash. The raids were put together quickly by the police in an effort to avoid being upended by the rumors that could spread like a forest fire. They were risky, and often turned down by other officers—but not Blythe.

He tapped his wet comb on the sink until it was dry. He exited the bathroom. Then he was out the door—and halfway across town only a few minutes later. Bledsoe's instructions were for him to park at the pharmacy and walk to meet him and the others. When Blythe arrived at Bledsoe's vague street briefing, another man they called Luke joined the raid simultaneously. The men introduced one another briefly before Bledsoe spoke.

"606 Ponderosa Lane. Be prepared, boys," Bledsoe said. "Surveillance hasn't seen the occupants leave. But it's now or never." Then he looked at the men and said, "All right, let's move in."

Shattered shards of door frame erupted into the foyer and the team of three passed through the flying splinters. Blythe heard a voice shout, "Aw, hell—*look out!*"

The exclamation sounded like a warning to someone else, leading them to believe there were at least two occupants within. Inside the door was a kitchen, with a table and three chairs—one empty, one still wobbling on the ground, and a third holding a tired, burly man with a leveled shotgun in his lap. The man made his choice clear, so Blythe stepped aside and Bledsoe returned aim at the seated man, firing two pistol shots. The chaired man squeezed off a round of buckshot a millisecond after Bledsoe's first bullet passed through his neck. The second bullet hit the man's chest, and he loosened his grip on the shotgun before it recoiled. More wood shattered next to Bledsoe's helmet. His first thought was that someone else had rammed through a different door, but he soon realized that the buckshot had hit the wood paneling by his head. Viciously, Bledsoe fired two more rounds into the disarmed man, who now lay on the floor.

The other men resumed operations, dusting off splinters and powder from their shoulders, and moving in deeper, with their guns drawn. Bledsoe saw the awe on the face of Blythe, and asked him to look over the bleeding man. Blythe stood over him, assessing the cowardice of the defeated man. He was bleeding out on the ground. As he lay dying, the last thing he saw before the devil took him was a beak-nosed man standing over him.

What happened to your nose?

Bledsoe and Luke rushed through the house, room by room, until they reached an open window in a back bedroom. They stood at the sill, looking out into the darkness—at the trampled grass that slowly began to stand upright again. They'd just missed him, the second occupant.

"I'll call in a unit to search the neighborhood," Bledsoe said. "We'll catch up to him." They turned and joined Blythe near the foyer.

"Everybody alright?" Bledsoe shouted from the hallway. He looked at the dead man on the ground when he entered the kitchen. Luke followed just behind.

"I think he's dead," Luke said, pointing to the man.

"No shit," Blythe said.

"I think that sonofabitch knew he was dead before we even showed up," said Bledsoe.

"Good shooting," Blythe said, and they all nodded.

"Now you know why I come in first," said Bledsoe, leaning against the wall and looking over the splintered void in the paneling. "Luke, call this in, will ya?"

"Sure. What about the other one?" Luke asked.

"Mention that too. Or you can chase him if you want," Bledsoe said.

"Hey I'm not worried—we got one and you're still alive. You mind if I split after I radio?" Luke asked.

"Nope," Bledsoe said. "Keep your eyes peeled when you leave."

"All right—well, don't stay out too late, men,"

Luke said and turned. He called dispatch from his cruiser at the pharmacy and drove home while Bledsoe and Jude Blythe remained at the scene. They stepped carefully around the evidence-covered table where the dead man had been sitting.

"You know the drill," Bledsoe said. "You can look around but don't touch anything until they come sweep the place."

Bledsoe was still leaning against the broken wall. Blythe stood opposite him in the foyer. They had been in other busts together before, but this was their first encounter that had nearly resulted in an officer fatality.

"Goddammit," Bledsoe said. "What a night ... goddammit. I suppose you're not gonna tag along anymore now that you've seen one of us shot at."

Blythe replied, "No ... no. Somebody's gotta make sure you don't get shot if you always go in first."

"And it sure isn't gonna be Luke," said Bledsoe.

"No. Heard his aim is terrible too."

"Who told you that? I guess there's probably some truth in that."

"How long before the sweepers get here, you think?" Blythe asked.

"At this hour? Who knows." Bledsoe looked over the dead man and the cash and drugs sprawled all over the table—hordes of plastic and a stainless steel scale.

They waited for some time, unconcerned. They

were each getting some form of hazard pay to talk and wait. Officers Bledsoe and Blythe discussed different obstacles in the way of advancing their careers—people they encountered who intended to injure them. They spoke of the risk and the pay—whether they were correlated precisely. They griped like traditional career men.

Appreciating the rapport in light of the events, Blythe said jokingly, "I'd take a beer."

"Help yourself, Jude," Bledsoe said, looking at the refrigerator.

They continued talking, and Bledsoe began to tell Blythe his stories of previous brushes with death. Blythe listened intently, with admiration. Blythe's interest fueled Bledsoe's willingness to talk. As he did, he sometimes exaggerated details, and eventually began to brag about things he'd encountered in his career. Once he started talking to the younger officers he sometimes had trouble stopping. He spoke of things that he had gotten away with—things considered to be "perks," which were not outlined formally and hardly spoken about. Bledsoe admitted that he and a few other officers would take money here and there from busts. Anyone who didn't feel comfortable taking cash kept their mouths shut anyway.

"When you're surrounded by men who you trust more than anyone—men who would risk their lives for you as you would for them, and who accept lethal risk in the name of public service, well. It's easy. All for a—let's be honest—*modest* paycheck. And it's always dirty money, anyway. No one misses a teeny tiny little bit of it. Nobody cares. Do you honestly think anyone does? You have to be smart—you just can't get greedy. Just teeny little amounts when it won't be noticed or missed. Nobody says anything. Nobody ever does."

Blythe didn't know how to respond. Initially he couldn't believe what he was hearing. He had rarely heard Bledsoe say so much, but that night was different. Even the air felt different. Everyone had heard rumors. But once Blythe heard it first-hand, he grew overjoyed. Bledsoe could tell.

"I use to lay in bed at night and picture stacks of cash all over the place," Bledsoe said. "In ovens and behind televisions. Empty boxes and hol-lowed-out walls." He pointed to the hole next to him. "Like teeny tiny bonuses—no, not bonuses. Deserved salaries, *owed* to us."

Blythe felt the adrenaline. He began to glance around the room carefully. His eyes became fixed on the splintered wood paneling near Bledsoe. Bledsoe turned and looked too. "How long you think we've been waiting?" Bledsoe asked, inter-rupting himself before he'd said too much. Maybe he already did.

"I don't know—maybe half an hour?" Blythe

responded. They began moving—both men anxiously circling the kitchen like buzzards, captivated.

Bledsoe moved closer and said, "Sweepers won't be here for at least another hour. Look … carefully *look*. Tell me if you see something, but don't touch anything. If anyone shows up, don't act stupid, okay?" Bledsoe covered his fingers with his shirt sleeve when he needed to use his hand to search. They leaned over the counter to look behind the refrigerator and stove, along the walls near the baseboards. There was nothing illegal about what they were doing just yet, that's how they justified it. They continued looking deliberately, not harming anyone or anything. Their search moved toward the other rooms, which were mostly barren too. They lifted a mattress and pulled open some drawers, careful to return anything they moved to how it had been. The place was a mess anyway.

They returned to the kitchen and stood looking things over one last time, eliminating every place they already looked. They did not speak and the room was still. Even the pool of glossy blood had stopped spreading and was beginning to darken on the floor below the dead man.

Blythe looked down at a woven jute rug that lay over the faux parquet floor near the body. Without speaking at all he noiselessly stepped over to the rug and slid it out of the way. The rug rolled and folded onto itself under the cabinet overhang. On the floor where the rug had been, a square with neatly cut edges could be seen among the surrounding floor tiles. Bledsoe saw where Blythe was headed and quickly jumped in to prevent him from messing something up. Bledsoe intervened and kneeled, trying to pry the lid open with his fingernails.

"It's like a goddamn paint can," Bledsoe said, softly. "Grab a knife." He pointed to a drawer. "Use your sleeve, Jude."

Blythe pulled his sleeve over his hand and opened the drawers furiously one by one and came back with a butter knife. Bledsoe used it to pry open the lid.

The aftermath of their entry—the dead man on the floor and the hole in the wall—it was all erased from their peripheral vision, eclipsed by their pulsing hearts and their ringing ears. With wide eyes, they saw that the empty space in the floor joist contained a shoe box. Inside that was a canvas bag containing two stacks of hundred dollar bills, as thick as a book banded together tightly.

"Bet that sonofabitch that bounced out the back window is gonna miss this," said Blythe.

"Hot skillet of hell ...would you look at that," Bledsoe said.

"Dogs Are Afraid
A Heights"

THE FOLLOWING MORNING, PERLIE FIN-
ished changing out a pulley and tightened it
up forcefully before stretching a fresh belt around
the grooves. He changed the oil and filter too.
He inspected his work carefully while the radio
played on, eventually returning the car to the lot
out front. It was almost too early for lunch but
Perlie decided that he was too hungry to start the
next repair.

"I'm running to the deli quick 'fore I start on
the next one," Perlie shouted toward Freddie, who
was sitting in the office. "Want anything?"

"Nope, I'm good," Freddie replied. "Thanks."

He came back and settled in at the multipur-
posed front counter. Sometimes, Freddie used the
edge of the counter as a footrest—the side that
wasn't stacked with repair manuals and trade

magazines. It also served as a breakroom table, on which either man ate hurriedly.

Perlie returned to the counter with a sandwich, and ripped the paper wrapping open. Freddie exited his office with the newspaper under his arm, folded with the sports section outward.

"Pastrami?" Freddie asked as he came in. He seated himself in one of the molded chairs across from Perlie. Perlie nodded, his mouth full of sandwich. Freddie went on. "Things going okay at the new place? No trouble or nothin'? Gettin' along fine so far?"

Perlie continued nodding and finished chewing. "Things are fine there, no trouble at all. Pretty quiet place, really."

"That's good, that's good," Freddie said, and ceased reading. It was obvious to Perlie that he wanted to talk. Freddie looked up at him. "You met anybody that's stayin' there? Makin' any friends?"

Perlie nodded no and spoke before taking another bite. "I see a man outside before I moved in. Haven't spoken to anyone yet though. It's mostly quiet after work. See Barb once in a while. She manages the place."

"Anybody else? I mean, like ... any women?" Freddie was grinning, but he appeared sincere. Perlie took a bite of his pastrami sandwich. He shook his head no. Freddie's hands were behind his head while he sat. He gave a vague look of disbelief and said, "Come on, kid, you can tell me. Give me somethin'."

Perlie finished chewing and replied, "Where'm I gonna meet women—these women you speak of?" He laughed with a mouth full of sandwich.

"Yeah, I don't know. Maybe you need a day off."

A man, who was a friend of Freddie's, entered the front door next to where Freddie was seated with the newspaper. The man pulled the door open and pulled himself into the front reception area in one fluid motion.

"Hey, hey! Look who it is." Freddie leaned forward from the chair and shook his friend's hand. "Perlie, this is Will."

Will gave a salute and Perlie said, "Pleasure, Will. You gotta pardon me—it's lunch time." He held up the sandwich.

"Workin' man's gotta eat when he can," Will said, casually.

"So, what we doin' to the ol' half-ton today, Will?" Freddie asked.

"You know—been twenty-five hundred miles since I last came in." Will shrugged.

"Oil, then. We can do it. We can do it, right Perlie? Today?"

"Yeah, yeah, 'course," Perlie said, trying to eat quickly.

"Set them keys down there on the counter," Freddie said. "Looks like Perlie's almost done anyhow. He'll take care of you." Will set the keys down and said, "Nice to meet you, Perlie."

"Have a seat," Freddie said. "Talk to your ol' pal Freddie. What you know?"

"Afraid I can't, Freddie boy," Will said. "Not today. Just wanted to drop the car off for you quick. And make sure you finally hired some help so you could get back to doin' what you do best."

"Oh yeah?" Freddie asked. "And what's that?"

"Sittin' on your ass, studyin' that sports page," Will said. The room filled with hearty laughter. Perlie finished eating and brushed his crumbs into the trash.

"Anyway, I can't stick around. Hell. My old lady's waitin' for me. She'll bring me back by later, alright?" Will looked at Perlie, who was standing now.

"No problem. Come back after five," Perlie said, and crossed back into to the garage bay.

Will watched Perlie leave and said quietly, "Say, Freddie, I got somethin' for you. Some new info from the track—an injury."

"Uh huh? Which horse?" Freddie asked, crossing his arms.

"Prince," said Will.

"No kiddin'?" Freddie asked. "He ain't gonna race?" Will's hands twitched outward as he shrugged. Freddie said, "Well, either way, I guess, it's helpful to know."

"Thought I'd share that with you. You goin' to

the track today, or just listenin' in?" Will's hand was on the door handle. His wife pulled up and waited for him in the lot.

"Goin' if I can," Freddie said. "You?"

"No—don't think so. But I'll surely be betting."

"Good—me too. Tell that ol' lady a yours to wish us luck." Freddie waved from inside the window.

Will opened the door and said, "Right. See you later."

Perlie was busy working when Freddie stepped into the doorway.

"I'm takin' off soon—you gonna be all right?" Freddie asked. "I'll be back by later, before you go home for the night."

"Yeah, Freddie. I'll be alright." Perlie continued to work.

"And listen," Freddie went on. "I got an important visitor tomorrow—forgot to tell you. A woman— she's comin' here to meet with me in my office. Not sure what time—she don't really give me much warning anymore." His voice sounded frustrated. "We'll visit in my office, but I probably won't intro- duce you. Nothin' personal, just business. But it's important. I just ask that you keep an eye on the counter while I'm meetin' with her, Perl."

"No problem," Perlie said, leaning beneath a light that hung from the opened hood of a car.

"Thanks, I know I can trust you Perl. And I'm doin' you a favor by not introducin' you, anyhow. She's a bit ... intimidating. Yeah, *intimidating*—that's the word. Women ... I tell you, Perl, some women are like wildcats. Always perched high, lookin' down on men. And us men—we the *dogs*, man. Cats prefer heights so they can look down on us dumb dogs. We just dumb dogs, Perl. And you know what?"

"What's that?" Perlie replied.

"Dogs are afraid a heights," Freddie said.

"They're afraid of cats, too," Perlie responded.

Freddie turned for his office and said her name out loud. It echoed softly through the hallway. *Uriella*.

As it turned out, Freddie was an individual like others obsessed with the *idea* of money, an individual who sought the chance to turn a little bit of it into a whole lot more. He played the horses, but at first seldomly and usually with some semblance of a strategy. The payout required no physical effort, no input—unlike the effort necessary to achieve marginal profits at the garage. He knew that racetracks and slot machines didn't get set up to pay out—but when they did, the feeling was unmatched. His attendance at the track became a habit, and then crossed over the line into obsession. Things got bad quick. When he did win he was really only climbing his way out of a hole that he had previously dug.

He found himself having to borrow to climb out of the hole, or he'd face foreclosure on the garage. Financing never proved to be easy for a Black man, let alone one with a felony. Autopia had been his livelihood, his wellbeing—the thing meant to deter lawlessness.

The money that kept him afloat came from a woman who only loaned to desperate people and only on the least favorable terms. In the den of thieves, moneylending is common practice. The woman who paid out, Uriella, took the deal, but needed help from another party to take on such a burden. The weariness grew for Freddie—and the distrust. Uriella and her partner, the financier, made Freddie transfer ownership of the garage. They threatened and intimidated him. Uriella reminded Freddie that she owned him and lately she had done so more frequently. Her hands dug deep into Freddie's pockets and she kept her eyes fixed on the sales at the garage. She was owed, and regretted ever involving herself with Freddie's money troubles to begin with. It had become a losing battle, waiting for a losing player to pay you back.

"Good Riddance to Bad Rubbish"

B LYTHE AND BLEDSOE SHARED THE SAME leader, Captain John Helene. He was a mustached man of stature and strength, his bright white hair suggesting the authority of inimitable wisdom. His career had begun in the military and afterwards reached a myriad of law divisions. He had an immense understanding of law and the crime that pushed back against it. In the middle of the two—crime and law—existed a place, a commingled area that any careered enforcer of the law was versed. Captain Helene knew of the dark alley deals and the turning of a blind eye, the give-and-take necessary for harmony when plain hard justice was inaccessible and hushed peace was realized instead.

His career proved his principles. Throughout it, he rarely missed a chance to strike down crime as he saw it—sometimes even before it occurred. Helene had a gift for recognizing premeditation—a misdeed gone unnoticed was rare, especially early in his career. Captain Helene saw publicized misconduct within law enforcement, before it was his burden to bear. It occurred in another town, district, or jurisdiction. Incidents of misconduct were sparse but highly publicized, destroying the trust of the citizens who expected outright protection above all else. There were more of these stories than had been brought to light, Captain Helene knew. Others knew too, but they remained tight-lipped, wanting to uphold the reputation of the law. Men of different virtues and ideals could still band together when they shared at least one rudimentary belief: the observed unity of law.

As a career in law and justice goes on, one finds misdeeds within the department to hardly be worth undertaking, knowing that an entire career can be undone from one such incident made public. But Helene knew of the temptations found early in a young policeman's career. Anytime he was informed of the possibility of an orchestrated test on the integrity of the men in his precinct, he whispered the information along to his peers.

The rumors of tests of honesty and integrity remained off-record and arrived as they often did, from the upper echelons, close to the office of the district attorney. Whenever the intelligence reached Captain Helene, the details were vague. The lack of context was a safeguard against conspiracy and coordination, preventing officers from knowing particulars.

Captain Helene and his comrades spoke quietly of tips, in an attempt to uphold law or their shared interpretation of it. He was contacted by the state attorney's office to meet with the district attorney for an exchange that would be as imperative as it was brief. And judging by the unofficial location, Helene could assume what would be discussed.

Outside of town at the fuel station not yet busy with travelers, Helene walked from his car to that of the district attorney, Donald Ellis. The air was cool and the sky appeared dark blue in the predawn. The minigolf course sat idle nearby. Standing outside, Captain Helene lowered his head to the passenger window. Donald looked up from the driver's seat at Helene and sat still, suggesting that he wasn't interested in cranking the window down.

"I'm gonna run in and get a coffee," Captain Helene said with extra emphasis through the closed window.

"Grab me today's paper," the district attorney responded. He wore a suit but kept the blazer laid neatly across the back seat. The center of the top of his skull was bald but he took pride in a neatly manicured beard.

Helene gave him a thumbs up and stepped into the filling station. It was still quiet at this hour. A semi hauling a trailer of hogs sat at the edge of the parking lot, its low diesel engine humming.

A few minutes later Captain Helene returned to the car with a folded newspaper under his arm and a steaming coffee in his hand. He climbed into Ellis's car and pulled the door shut. Helene handed Ellis the folded newspaper.

"Thanks," Ellis responded. "I've just got a minute so I'll cut right to the chase, John. This is one of those moments when I tell you to keep your nose clean, got me?"

Captain Helene nodded. He took a sip of his coffee.

"There's a great deal of pressure now. With all that, what happened in Beacon," Ellis said and pointed to the newspaper, referring to a recently debauched investigation. "I'm sure you already know. Anyway the point is we can't have any more of *that*. And if any of *that* type of behavior is happening here in your precinct, we'll know about it soon enough. Do you understand, John?"

"It won't be a problem, Don," Helene said and took another sip, careful not to burn his tongue. "Good riddance to bad rubbish, I always say."

"Yeah, whatever. Thanks for the paper. Now, if you'll excuse me, I've got to get to work."

Captain John Helene climbed out of the car,

taking with him his coffee and the newly received information.

Rumors of corruption brought about a reckoning from above—a push to identify all cases of police misconduct and to publicly convict those responsible. For the office of the district attorney, identifying and eliminating corrupt police officers and administration was a display of integrity—a chance at regaining trust by eliminating as many anecdotes of corruption as possible. The district attorney, Donald Ellis, thought that maybe one bad tale would be the outcome of an integrity test but likely no more than one singular example would be all that was necessary to make the point that all parties needed to watch their step. One bad headline—a story. Surely this was enough to show the district attorney's seriousness for eradicating corruption. Nothing wrong with firing a few bad officers on the way to redemption—all without digging too deeply, or uncovering the wrongdoing that since made its way to the top.

The minions of the district attorney's office made hushed comments to their cohorts about their intentions to eliminate at least the *perception* of corruption. Typically, misconduct was uncovered when money was planted at a crime scene. The money was left there as bait, with the intention of exposing internal corruption—it was called an integrity test. Just the *possibility* of a test had proven to be a deterrent in its own right, keeping all who suspected it on their best behavior. Detectives and patrolmen went into each situation wondering if it had been fabricated to catch a dirty cop. This time, however, in light of recent events and mounting pressure, Donald Ellis had instructed agents to actually place money—an integrity test—at a scene to be investigated. He ruminated what might be uncovered.

"Want Me to Dress Up Like a Clown?"

FREDDIE HAD SPENT ENOUGH TIME ON THE unjust side of a deal. His inability to change the arrangement, his complacency in the unfairness of acting as the one who stands to lose, made the situation perpetually insurmountable. His inability to climb out of the hole that Uriella was keeping him in caused him to lack judgment.

He'd been stealing from Uriella for some time—underreporting sales at the garage and betting what he owed her at the track so that he could earn it all back and then some, so that he could walk away from it all. He had become reckless. Uriella's suspicion had been confirmed since her last visit—the day that Perlie started, and the day he noticed her fancy coupe out front on the street.

Freddie was constantly under the thumb of Uriella after she coerced him into signing the garage over. He'd done all right covering for himself so far, becoming skillful at creating excuses to avoid her accusations. But he was finding it increasingly hard to keep her away from the garage. This, he never took as a good indicator. Knowing he would lose the shop anyway if he failed to pay her back, he stood by his choice to bravely face her.

The day that Uriella arrived at the garage, the air held a nostalgic late-summer chill. Perlie was settling into his new life and his new surroundings; his sudden routine. Freddie was dressed in an ironed shirt, and he had shaved, too. He had on shiny loafers and khakis—a departure from his usual free-form demeanor.

Uriella pulled along the curb, her silver coupe reflecting the bright morning sky. She entered Autopia through the front door and walked immediately to Freddie's office, right past Perlie, before he could answer the question that she didn't bother to ask. Because, by now, she had known exactly where Freddie could be found. Unless he was at the track, of course.

Perlie saw her haste. Now he knew that Uriella was the cat that Freddie spoke of, perched above. Her allure was obvious, and because her intimidation was inherent, it allowed her to move through the world effortlessly. Her prey rarely even tried to escape.

She entered Freddie's office, where he was seated, awaiting her arrival anxiously.

"Uriella," Freddie said quickly.

"Freddie. I haven't the time today. Please open the safe."

"Okay, wait—"

"No. I can't wait. I won't wait. Do you understand me? Open the safe." Freddie hesitated and she spoke again. "Open it, or move aside and tell me the combination, Freddie. Either way, I'll get into the safe."

"Not all the slips are in there," Freddie said.

"Where are they, Freddie?"

"—and I just went to the bank."

"Then I'll need that deposit slip too. Open the safe, Freddie." Uriella pursed her lips. "Open the safe. Open the safe willingly or not—but make a decision before I make it for you."

"Okay, okay—no problem," Freddie conceded. He knelt on the floor like an altar boy at the safe. He turned the dial counter-clockwise to clear the mechanism and then he spun it to each number carefully. He was overthinking things because of her vigilance. Freddie froze on the last number of the safe combination. His heart raced and he sensed Uriella's indignation. He started the combination over—this time he spun the dial with whimsy. He tried to pretend he was alone, without her eyes burning the back of him.

Freddie's guilt was exposed.

"Yes? Is there a problem?" Uriella asked.

She already knows. Freddie thought about the money and the track. He did his best to calmly restart the combination. Once again, he spun the dial to clear the lock mechanism, spinning it three times counterclockwise but missing the starting number this time. Freddie cleared the dial once more. It was now the third time. His back was to Uriella, so she couldn't see his distressed face. He chewed his lip.

Finally, he spun the dial all the way through until the mechanism clicked on the last number. He turned the door handle and pulled open the safe door. The bolts ejected again once the door was open, so that the steel cylinders were exposed at the door's edge. Freddie turned and looked at Uriella standing before him in his office. He struggled to read her expression.

"Hand me the invoices," she said, and took a seat. "And the cash, too."

"I told you—I already went to the bank."

"But surely you have accepted cash today, and you haven't yet taken it to the bank?"

"But it ain't in here, yet," Freddie said.

"Where is it, then?" she asked.

"In the drawer under the front counter. I can go and get it."

"You should've said that, then—that today's

cash is in the drawer. Give me answers, not problems. Better yet—give me solutions."

Freddie turned and handed her an unorganized pile of invoices, and then turned and cleared a few others from the inside the safe. He handed her all the invoices that he could find while she waited, patiently seated with her legs crossed.

"Freddie—these are all of your invoices?"

"Yes."

"Let me look at your deposits—I'll need to check the totals." Freddie reached into his desk and handed her a book of carbon-copied deposit slips. She took them but didn't look at them closely. Her eyes remained fixed on Freddie.

Finally, he said, "Oh,"—realizing that she would need his calculator to add the amounts.

Ten minutes passed excruciatingly, while Uriella totaled the sales at Autopia. She reconciled and matched invoice totals to deposits going all the way back to her last visit. The calculator clicked furiously while Freddie watched, trying hard not to fidget. He began to feel thirsty and began to stand up, saying, "I'm gonna get a drink of water."

"No," she said. "Sit." So he did.

She tallied totals on a notepad and said, "You are still aware of our arrangement, Freddie?" Her head was still down, her fingers clicking furiously. Freddie nodded. He knew he was in deep. "And no one gave you any reason to think otherwise?" she asked.

"No," he said. Then Freddie tried to explain before Uriella could even ask why the deposits had been decreasing over time—why they were often less than the daily ticket totals. He argued that he had only recently hired Perlie, and before hiring him, he had been working alone, and so he couldn't always take as many jobs as he'd like. He explained as best he could and apologized again and again. Freddie had gotten good at that. He told her, he'd hired a mechanic now, so he could take on more work and get the sales back up.

Uriella recognized that Freddie was lying—that he was bending the truth to fit the narrative. He went on explaining, rarely pausing or allowing her to even speak. She let this go on awhile before finally planting the papers and calculator back on his desk. She cut him off abruptly.

"Freddie," she said.

He was still explaining himself, but he paused. "Yeah?"

"Do you know how I know you are lying to me?" she asked.

"Somethin' not addin' up?" Freddie looked anxiously at the mountain of paper slips.

"Of course not. But that's not how I know that you are lying. I *know* that you are lying because you are going on and on about why the sales are off."

"Yeah?" Freddie failed to follow.

"Before I've even addressed the sales," she said.

"And, you've got this look like you're more interested in my reaction than anything else. Do you know why I think that is?"

"Why?" Freddie said. He hated the way Uriella made him feel—the way she patronized him every time she came around the garage. He acknowledged things had gotten worse quickly.

"Because people who are preoccupied with convincing others are really only speaking to convince *themselves*."

"Okay, Uriella," he said, defeatedly.

"It is apparent that I can no longer count on you to keep a steady flow or revenue—per our arrangement."

"I'll fix it. I could paint the building—clean the place up a bit. If I could hire another mechanic to take on more jobs, maybe then? You name it, Uriella. What should I do? What you want me to do? Want me to dress up like a clown? Spin a sign out on the street for customers to see?" Freddie was panicking.

"Ha. How do you expect to trust me—to trust that I will even allow this business to go on like this if I cannot trust you?"

"I ..."

But Uriella was already standing and leaving. She looked into the garage at Perlie as she glided past the door. But now he was working—intentionally trying to avoid her, as Freddie had asked. Perlie didn't see Uriella leave.

"Lord's Refuge, My Ass"

GENE HAD DARK FORLORN EYES, POS-
sessing the look of a boy who'd become a
man too quickly—stripped of his innocence,
which had been replaced by a sorrowful weight.
He was a slender man whose bronze skin wrapped
tightly around his bones, knobs and humps pro-
truding as he walked. His shoulders rolled like a
wildcat and he was agile like one, too. Especially
when his back was against a wall. Troubled but
independent, Gene lived his life like a lone beast
scurrying about in the night—a true master of eva-
sion. He was known by many criminals vaguely
for one reason or another but cops knew very little
about him and he intended to keep it that way.

Gene had been at the bust that night, at 606
Ponderosa, sitting in a chair at the kitchen table
with the burly man who was now dead. Gene had

been handing him cash he'd collected as they both counted, just before police busted in and shot the other man through the neck. He heard the shots ring out from the back of the apartment as he bolted out the window undetected. And he left without getting his split. The man with the shotgun in his lap, Milt, was counting out Gene's commission but Gene never had a chance to keep it because he had heard someone outside the door and by the time he reached the hallway he heard the door frame crack and splinter when the cops busted in. Gene acted in that moment purely by criminal instinct, bolting faster than the cops could swing the door open. Though he left without his share, his split second decision allowed him to leave with his life which was more than he could say about Milt. A life belongs to the person who gets to keep it but money doesn't belong to anyone. It only belongs to the person who holds it, but once they let go, it's anybody's.

Gene had relied on the dead man to supply him with the stuff that he pushed out into the streets. He made a cut of it. And like Freddie, Gene had had to rely on the woman, Uriella, for money here and there—small amounts that he could pay back quickly after he was paid out. Usually it worked out quickly and Uriella wouldn't make him pay back the interest, instead assigning him a petty errand each time he owed her.

Gene was square with Uriella now, though. He didn't owe her a dime. So the arrangement between the two of them was new for both of them. She'd ask him to do her dirty work and would pay him in return. He like it better this way, not really ever feeling indebted. Now, he was out all of the money that he should have been paid by Milt before the cops busted in and shot the place up. Uriella's timing was impeccable. Gene needed cash quick and Uriella needed something taken care of.

She paid Gene to eliminate her latest problem: distrust. Distrust now irreconcilable and held with pure spite for the man who not only owed her a great deal of money but had the nerve to continue taking from her while he lied about it. Gene already knew who Freddie was. They had been acquainted through criminal encounters. Gene was better at bolting when he needed to— better at knowing when the paths to freedom were disappearing. He always kept sight of an exit and did his best to avoid relying on anyone so much that his own freedom was in jeopardy.

Now it was on, and Freddie knew he was in trouble but didn't expect to what degree Uriella would counteract, the lengths she was prepared to go to pacify her never ending hemorrhaging of money caused by Freddie. Freddie, the liar. Freddie, the gambler. The cheater and the stealer, Freddie. After Gene went out into the moonlit streets that first time looking for Freddie with his blade ready, he returned ineffective. Regretfully, he couldn't locate the man who he had been instructed to eliminate. In the car as he drove, Gene could feel the utter electricity that this new errand brought. This was easily the most severe task that Uriella had ever put on him.

Returning home after coming up empty handed, Gene rounded the corner up the street from his block, and observed two men who lingered in the shadows outside his apartment window. One of them moved his head around slowly and peered through the window. Gene slowly passed by, seeing the side of one of the men's faces as it moved toward the glass. He saw the stocky physique of the other man, who had his back to the street. Neither of them he recognized. But both of them were armed with holsters on their sides. *How strange*, Gene thought. It appeared that they were looking for him, or someone, but apparently lacked some authority to enter. They seemed concerned with his apartment and what was inside—or who they were expecting to find there. Gene continued to drive down the street past his place until his place was out of sight. He sat forward, with his head over the steering wheel, his car creeping but his mind racing. He was already planning his exit.

That's it—I've been made somehow. A hired murderer. And once again I'll have to give up my cut. Because

*now my bounty—for Uriella's errand—is inaccessible.
But it won't matter because I'll probably go to jail
anyway. The cops must know. Someone told them. Maybe
she set me up. But why? I needed the money and she convinced me to do it but failed to protect me. Maybe she set
me up. She must have. But I haven't done anything yet.
He's still alive. They can't arrest me. I need to get back
inside and get my goddamn money.*

He couldn't go back home just yet, so, Gene
hit the main drag for several miles and eventually,
after gathering his nerve, stopped off at a phone
booth at a pump station to call Uriella. Gene figured she'd probably assume he was calling to tell
her that the job was done, or that he was calling to
confirm that Freddie was dead. But, that's not why
he was calling. He needed to know why two armed
men were at his door just now.

Back at Gene's place, under cover of darkness,
two men had been tasked with planting money,
on behalf of the state police's internal affairs divi-
sion. They'd been instructed to move in quickly
after determining that the apartment was vacant.
The plan was to dump the money that they'd
been supplied, to place it inside, some place where
responding officers would find it.

The first agent—a short stocky man who had
previously been recruited for such tasks—had no
trouble prying the door open, carefully disengaging

the lock using a flat bar. He gained entry with ease. The other agent—a bland and hairless middle-aged man carrying a canvas duffle bag—followed him into Gene's empty apartment. Once inside, they moved hastily and only by flashlight. Their movement appeared choreographed while they cleared rooms and closets, rotating their rigid bodies with guns and flashlights drawn.

Once they determined that they were alone, they quickly carried out their orders and planted the state-provided test money at their discretion. With a glance, the bald, agent of internal affairs, noticed an item suitable for concealing the planted money—a biblical effigy coated with aged paint; a statue of Jesus. He began to reach for it, his fingertips inches away, when the other, more stout officer whispered, "No!"

He was more bullheaded, and decided the statue was both too obvious and too concealing. So they left it alone. The hiding spot had to be just right—both subtle and forthright. That was the trouble, it always was—striking the balance. Time ticked on and their position became increasingly vulnerable inside the apartment. The occupant might arrive at any moment. The stocky officer of internal affairs decided on a different idea, kneeling next to the bed near the mattress opposite the effigy. He had the bald officer empty the canvas bag onto the floor. Then he carefully stacked the bundles of cash between the box spring and mattress.

They exited in unison—confidently and without haste.

The internal affairs duo drove down the street, past decrepit houses unlit by broken streetlights, and wound their way to a payphone. Insects swarmed in the buzzing light from above. They parked and the stocky agent grabbed change from his pocket and fed the payphone. He held the receiver to his ear and dialed 911. They had developed a plausible reason for the call, having heard that there had been a bust just days ago that resulted in a fatality. They also read in the report that someone had evaded arrest by sneaking out through a back window and so they chose a known associate to Milt with a criminal record and arrived at his doorstep. Gene's inclusion in the predicament, the integrity test, was merely by happenstance.

"Yes, I have some information about a crime ... there was a drug bust on Ponderosa ... somebody got shot and killed and ... somebody got away, I know who it was ... he lives at 4000 Simshaw."

Officer Bledsoe responded to an anonymous phoned-in tip relating to the previous night's bust. Blythe accompanied him. When they arrived, they discovered an empty but disorderly apartment. They knew who allegedly lived there, according to the tip, and the mail on the counter inside verified the name. They assumed, this man, Gene, who was an accomplice of the man shot and killed at the Ponderosa shoot-out, to indeed be the one who snuck out through the back window, evading police. What they didn't know was that it was only by chance, (and unfortunate luck, for Gene), that he had been connected to the Ponderosa address. The connection was fabricated by the officers of internal affairs, only in an effort to pick a plausible locale to set up the proposed sting—the integrity test.

They looked around carefully for anything tying the man to the scene. But both Officers Blythe and Bledsoe knew what else they were looking for, too. Same as before, just looking—nothing illegal about it, not harming anyone or anything. *Just looking.* A quick check beneath the kitchen rug revealed nothing. They moved on to the cluttered bedroom. Now, for the second time, strangers were jumbling around in Gene's empty bedroom. Blythe and Bledsoe, too, noticed the bed and the end tables on either side of it—cluttered with matchbooks, empty plastic bottles, and cups filled partially with liquid.

On one end table stood the plaster statue of Jesus, the biblical effigy that was readily dismissed earlier. Blythe noticed the colorfully ornate surface of it, worn with time. The face of the effigy gazed slightly off center, just past the officers.

The flesh-toned paint was chipped and discolored and wavy chestnut hair flowed down to the robed shoulders—the robe itself lackluster gold with red edges. A fine amount of dirt had accumulated in the narrow crevices of the statue, but much of the surface remained unblemished. Flowing like the hair, the robe hung down and fanned out at the base, barely revealing two feet standing atop a wooden pentagon box thick with varnish. The box below was flat and wide and no more than a few inches deep. The religious display was incongruous. It was indeed, an obvious oddity in the bedroom. Blythe sneered, his eyes aligning with the face of the statue, sitting only a couple feet tall, as it sat on the end table. He lifted it by the waist, careful to avoid nicking the head as he turned it.

That rush—the one Blythe had felt before, was beginning to overtake him again. He narrowed his eyes and tapped his foremost knuckle on the bottom of the pentagon box. He knocked on one side, too. The hollow knocks were noisy in the quiet bedroom. Blythe looked at Bledsoe with delight. Blythe carefully flipped the statue back upright and, unprompted, Bledsoe held his hands caringly beneath it, like he was ready to catch an infant as it was being delivered. Blythe pried the base of the box open with one hand.

What a curious sight—two officers of the law

acting like thieves, shaking down the Son of Man, all in the shadow of bleeding corruption.

The lid made a pop and went flying onto the dirty carpet floor. The contents came out, too—the men flailed, trying to catch it all. They looked at the sharp-edged shapes in the darkness, spewed onto the floor below them. Banded stacks of hundred dollar bills, laid on the carpet like dice on a felted game table.

Gene returned home sometime later, after more deliberation. He parked and grabbed the knife that he'd brought with him earlier. Gingerly, he approached his place. Moving his head quickly, he scanned the surroundings outside the apartment. He pressed his ear firmly to the door until all outdoor noise was muted, then he listened. When he couldn't make out any noise from inside through the door, he gripped the door handle and turned the key, entering his apartment.

The place appeared exactly as he had left it. Any strangeness that he felt surrounding him was only due to what he observed *outside* the apartment. He proceeded, looking inside of cabinets and drawers, shuffling items around as if he, too, were looking for something. His mind continued racing. Had those men even entered? Would they come back? Were they waiting for him now? What were they after, anyway? The questions appeared faster than he could address them. Gene failed to remember exactly where things had been left before he departed, where items sat and how they were positioned. But, everything looked in order now. No one must have come in, after all. Then, what was the point?

Gene saw the effigy on the bedside table and thought of the payment for Uriella's latest errand. Was that what they were after? It couldn't be. He turned the statue upside down and pried open the box at the foot of the statue. Nothing came out, now. It was empty.

Panicked and in disarray, he rushed into the kitchen and reached for the phone to call Uriella. He didn't know what else to do. The line rang several times before she finally answered.

"Hello," Uriella said calmly.

"It's Gene."

"The job—it is done?"

"No … I tried to call you and tell you."

"When?"

"Earlier. From a payphone."

"Then what is it? What are you calling me for if you haven't yet done the job you were paid to do?"

"I tried calling you before but now it's somethin' else. The money that you paid me—well … it's gone."

"Gone? How? What do you mean? Where was

it? I'm not responsible for your negligence, do you understand?"

"I hid it—the day you gave it to me."

"Where?"

"It doesn't matter. Or maybe it does. But really what matters is that it was somewhere hidden, and then—"

"And then what?" Uriella's voice grew with anger.

"It's strange—just listen. Earlier I went to find him … er, to run the errand. I came up empty-handed. He wasn't at the garage or at home. I figured he was at the track, which doesn't do me any good, so anyway, it was getting' late and I came back to my place. But when I pulled down the street, I saw two men—"

"Are you telling a story? Because if you are, if you are lying …"

"No, no, listen. Two men, they appeared to be cops but … they looked like they were lookin' for me."

"How do you know? Did you talk to them?"

"No, they were lookin' through my windows to see if I was home."

"To arrest you?"

"No. I mean, I don't think so. They looked like they were just lookin' for me. Or, like they were lookin' to make sure I was gone. It gave me a weird feeling. I had a weird feeling, like someone tipped them off about the job—this errand. Then I tried to call you to ask you—"

"To ask me what? If I called the police and set you up?" Uriella spoke sharply.

Gene hesitated. "How else would they know?"

"Know what? Where you live? Anyone can find that out, don't be stupid."

"They knew where I put the money that you gave me … It's gone."

"Gone? How? This is not my problem. Surely you must have told someone where you put the money. Where *did* you put the money, Gene? How do you know no one saw you hide it?"

"I was careful. No one saw me hid it. I can't afford to lose this money. I'm already out, from before … Anyway, I hid it next to my bed. In a statue … of Jesus. And I was alone when I hid it. I didn't tell anyone. No one saw me. I hid it quick and then I left to look for you-know-who."

"*Jesus?* Jesus. You must carry on with the plan. It still needs your attention." Uriella was more irritated now. She knew why Gene was really calling. "I suppose you think that you need to get repaid?"

"Well, yes—if I'm still gonna do it, I'm owed," Gene said carefully.

"You are not owed," Uriella shot back. "You *will* be owed when the thing for which I have paid you, in good faith before the job was even done, is *done.*"

"Yes, of course. You're right," Gene agreed.

"But if this is some sort of scheme to double your payment ... well, when it comes to men trying to take me for a ride, I am in no particular mood. Surely you understand the consequences if that is the case."

"I promise you, I have been robbed," Gene pleaded. "Or, so it seems."

"So it seems. Tell me about these two men— you said they were cops?"

Gene described what he had witnessed on the street. Uriella listened from a reclined position on her patio, seated in a teak lawn chair, jotting down the details on the back of a napkin atop an acrylic table at her side. The phone was held tight between her soft cheek and her effortlessly posed shoulder as she wrote. She was calmer now.

"Is that all?" she asked.

"I didn't see much. I was worried they would see me so I kept movin'. Should I leave? Leave town? You think someone knows about the job?"

"It isn't possible unless you told someone, which you said you did not."

"Then how did—"

Uriella cut him off. "A coincidence perhaps. I do not know. The intruders, the missing money, the statue ... of Jesus. If someone knew ... or a cop, even—"

Gene was thinking. "They looked like cops,"

he said. "The way they were standing, strapped with guns."

"Maybe. But they were not acting as law enforcement should, were they? Cops don't wait for people to leave and take their money, do they?" Uriella took a sip from the glass at her side.

"Guess not," Gene agreed.

"You guess not. I don't either. I'll get you your money but this time not until the job is done. And, Gene?"

"Yeah?"

"This will be the last time. Keep it somewhere safe. Safer than *Jesus*."

"Of course." Gene agreed.

The line clicked dead. Gene placed the telephone back on the receiver and stared at it. Then he said, "Lord's refuge, my ass."

"Some Piece of Rubbish That Deserves to be Locked Up Anyway"

O FFICERS BLEDSOE AND BLYTHE WERE called into the office of their precinct captain, Captain John Helene, first thing in the morning. They each were burdened with fear that the cash they took from the effigy box had somehow been made known to the captain. Their greediness had quickly surpassed even their own expectations.

They arrived separately and made their way to the precinct in a frenzied panic. They thought about the few inconceivable ways that the captain could have discovered their crime so quickly. If their theft was known, as they both now suspected, the knowledge stopped at the captain—if the money were *truly* an integrity test, they likely would have both been arrested by now. Instead, they were asked to return to the precinct voluntarily. Either way fate was waiting inside.

They stepped through the door in tandem and entered Captain Helene's office. His shades were drawn and the Captain's face seemed strange and disillusioned. "Have a seat." He waved his hand toward the chairs as the officers entered. Then he sat, too. Blythe and Bledsoe avoided the urge to exchange glances and instead focused on the captain, doing their best to appear innocent.

"As you may have heard, some money was indeed planted by the state at a locale—a place where you two were led on a *fake* tip." Captain Helene looked away, fearing that he might recognize guilt in the eyes of either officer.

"However, I'm told that the agents who planted the money returned to the house right after watching you two depart." He pointed at both men with two fingers of the same hand. "And as it turns out, that money, the integrity money … remained exactly as they had left it—untouched beneath a mattress in one of the bedrooms."

Officer Blythe and the other exchanged vague looks of alarm, careful to not appear incriminating in any manner. The captain proceeded.

"What I find odd—and they do too—is that you stated that you both searched the scene for anything that might have tied that man to that jam-up at Ponderosa. But you hardly found anything—not even the money that they wanted you to find and turn in as evidence. You didn't take it … *and* you didn't turn it in."

Blythe felt the blood empty from his face. Bledsoe, noticing his discomfort, chimed in quickly. "That was my fault, Captain," he said. Blythe glanced at him briefly as Bledsoe went on speaking. "We knew the occupant wasn't home and we were in a rush, working as quickly as possible, per my instruction, to make sure that we could get out before this man—"

"—from the Ponderosa jam, allegedly," Blythe added, focusing the attention back on the lie that the state told to bring them to Gene's place on Simshaw in the first place. Bledsoe had his back and now Blythe felt that he needed to reciprocate.

"Yeah, we rushed through the place, before that suspect returned home and caught the two of us in there, without backup or anything." Bledsoe looked at Blythe again. "We—and I think the state, too—assumed the guy wasn't coming back, or that he would be there to begin with so we could take him in for questioning. But we couldn't know for sure, so I hurried us."

The captain bought the story. "I see. At the end of the day, I suppose it doesn't matter much, because the money remained anyway. Had either of you taken it—well … you both know, I think."

"Yes, captain," Officer Bledsoe said.

Blythe agreed. "Yes, of course."

"You two—keep it clean, okay? And follow up on this Simshaw guy. He does have a record, ties to that operation at Ponderosa. Other than that, we don't know much about him. No one really knows if he was the guy that escaped out the window. But, you need to look into it. Anyway, we're all done here."

The officers stood and exited into the hall.

After turning the first corner, walking down the corridor at the precinct, Blythe whispered to Bledsoe, "Is this a set up? I don't—"

"Shut your damned mouth," Bledsoe responded sharply. He tried to remain calm. "I don't know."

They walked on, and Blythe said, hushed, "Then whose money was it?"

"I don't know, Jude!"

Blythe and Bledsoe headed straight for the Piñon Pub after work to decompress the afternoon's chaos over a drink.

They sat opposite one another in a wobbly booth and spoke quietly, still concerned with the prospect that they were somehow being set up. The inside of the bar was quiet but the air felt conspiratorial. Bledsoe offered Blythe a cigarette but he waved his hand dismissively. Blythe was drinking a pilsner. Bledsoe went straight for whisky.

"We need to dump the money," Blythe said. "You still have yours?"

"Of course—what do you think? What would I

do with it?" Bledsoe was growing irritated but felt it was imperative that he and Blythe get on the same page. "But … I agree. Someone's gonna come looking for that money. I just don't know who. We need to put it on someone else. Plant it just like the state tried to do to us."

"Who do you think it belongs to if the state didn't plant it?"

"I don't know. It can't belong to *nobody*. And we can't wait around until they find out we have it. Or then … we're made."

"We need to dump it—the money."

"I know, goddammit!" Bledsoe said. A drunk at the bar turned and looked at them.

Blythe pressed his back hard into the booth, hoping it would swallow him so he could disappear. He took a deep breath. "Let's just dump it somewhere … somewhere where it belongs. You said it—the money's dirty." Blythe sounded nervous. He hoped to come up with a solution that didn't annoy Bledsoe.

"What if the police find it first? Or what if the serial numbers are recorded?"

"*The police* already have it," Blythe said, pointing at themselves. He regretted the comment immediately.

Bledsoe barely looked up from his glass and said, "You know what I mean, goddammit."

They both took a drink to let the idea soak.

"The place where the cash could be dumped—like you said, *where it belongs*," Bledsoe said frantically.

"Where some poor crook will take it, no questions asked," said Blythe.

"Poor fellas like us," said Bledsoe. He was angry for his greed, and angry at Blythe for feeding it.

"Yeah, I guess. Just have to make sure it gets found, even though it's gotta look—"

"Like it wasn't supposed to be found," Bledsoe said.

"Exactly."

"We'll leave the cash somewhere where some piece of rubbish that deserves to be locked up anyway will find it."

"They'll find it and take it for themselves, and if they spend it on drugs or something and get busted, it won't matter. If it's marked like you said and someone comes asking questions when it shows up on the radar again, they'll blame the crook."

"We just gotta make sure that crook isn't us. So, where Jude? Where do we leave it?" Bledsoe was relying on Blythe to get them out of the mess he had helped them into.

"We need a car," said Blythe.

"I've *got* a car," Bledsoe responded.

"Not like that. One that won't be missed. For putting the money in. Trust me."

"A car that might be of interest to somebody

else?" Bledsoe leaned in across the booth. "You're suggesting we *steal* a car?"

"Precisely," Blythe said, impressed now by his own sudden onset of wisdom under pressure.

Officers Blythe and Bledsoe brought their stashes together and carefully faced the bills, and then re-banded them in the same manner they were when they were found inside the hollow box beneath the plaster statue of Jesus. The King of Kings, Lord of Lords. *The Son of Man.* They made a plan to dump the bounty off on someone else, thus absolving themselves. And if the state was tracking the bills, after all, they would came down on whoever took the money next, after they dumped it. And if the criminal that took the bait lied, it wouldn't matter. Every investigator knows that a crook always denies involvement anyway.

Bledsoe was tasked with locating and stealing a car to be used in their scheme of disassociation. After all, he was the more veteran officer, so he took on the role knowing that then it would get done right. He chose a neighborhood where he considered crimes commonplace anyway. Officer Bledsoe was versed in thinking like a criminal. He wondered if a cop's preponderance for criminal behavior, throughout his career in law enforcement, could bring a virtuous officer just close enough to criminality that stepping over the line was inevitable. Bledsoe didn't think any officer, or anyone for that matter, had *only* purely honest thoughts and behaviors. At some point, everyone underwent a criminal daydream, at the very least. Even if the daydream was never carried out, he wondered if that person could still be considered honest. Maybe that was justification. He concealed his own failed integrity by surrounding himself with others he considered lawfully corrupt. Recruiting other naive officers, he blurred the line.

And so it took very little for Bledsoe to convince Blythe, earlier at the Piñon Pub, that it was necessary to follow the mechanic from the garage to his home. They were counting on the mechanic, who worked at the garage that employed criminals, to take the money. Blythe had already known about Autopia from his unplanned visit earlier— when he dropped off his mother's Oldsmobile. But Blythe knew very little about the mechanic who helped him at the counter that day. So, the mechanic was followed.

When Perlie, unaware, reached the halfway house complex after work, he waved to Barb who was heading home for the day. Then he disappeared behind the main office and ducked in through the door to his unit. Blythe was trying hard to focus on Perlie and was not looking forward as he coasted along the street in his car. Barb, on her way to pick up her daughter, began crossing the street on foot and was nearly hit by Blythe's car.

She shouted just as he noticed her crossing before him. He smashed his foot into the brake pedal abruptly, missing which unit Perlie entered. Barb exclaimed and gave Blythe a chilling look before walking on. Perlie was already inside his unit at the halfway house and was oblivious to the exchange. Blythe parked somewhere on the street and went up to peer through the glass of one of the units that he thought Perlie might have entered, just to confirm. He stood in the trodden grass along the foundation of the apparently vacant unit. Through the window, he noticed that the kitchen was empty. Blythe slid around to another window and saw the rooms destitute, failing to consider what little a parolee has immediately after release. The unit he was looking at was empty, after all. Blythe scratched his head, eventually deciding that the building he was looking into was vacant and that Perlie must have entered the adjacent one. In broad daylight, he nearly checked the other building but changed his mind quickly when another occupant of the halfway house, seated in a patio chair outside, noticed Blythe and abruptly stood, watching him concernedly. Blythe quickly bailed. His inference was futile, his judgment wrong, and his failure wouldn't go without consequence.

Bledsoe arrived at the shoddy car to be used as the decoy. It was parked at the side of a dark street, defenseless. He scoped his surroundings, cautiously approaching the car while he pulled a flat bar from his jacket and slipped it in past the weather stripping at the passenger window with ease. He breached the door from a kneeling position, leaning against the car in the dark, and turned, sliding his body into the car and over the console into the opposite seat. He took out a small leather pouch and set it on his lap, using the flashlight in his mouth to locate the rake and hook of the right size. Like a focused surgeon, he slid the tiny pick into the ignition with ease.

He turned the ignition without failure—setting in motion, irrevocably, the plan that would exonerate him of his wrongdoing. But only through criminality could he arrive at his innocence. The shame bore down on Officer Bledsoe.

A cold but principled Uriella determined that the money that she had given Gene had not yet technically belonged to him. It wouldn't belong to him until he had murdered her unruly borrower, Freddie. It belonged to *her*. By now, she had grown more irritated than expected. She felt like her money was disappearing all around her—either intentionally or coincidentally. Freddie had been stealing from her for some time and she would be damned if the bounty for his murder would cost her twice the originally agreed upon amount.

She used her insight into police informants

from previous dealings to receive information—the kind of intelligence that passes among criminals with ease. For Uriella, the line dividing crime and virtue had always been blurred.

Through an informant, she discovered almost immediately the rumors of state agents planting money to ensure trustworthiness in the precinct—though the tests were said to be more about the public's confidence than the state agency that advocated for it. This was hardly her concern at first, but she investigated further, pressing a police informant here and another there, gathering dirt on all of them as she went along. The contacts led her to a conversation with one source who told her that someone inside the force was warning other cops about anonymous phone calls and fake situations luring officers into a trap. Uriella was told that the officer was bragging about how he and another officer had been lured to a scene but didn't take anything, thereby passing the integrity test. *How virtuous.* But what was odd, the informant told Uriella, was that he had known the officer and had heard him boast about skimming money from evidence in the past. The informant had even seen it firsthand, though he denied ever having partaken himself.

Uriella asked for the name of the officer. And like everything she asked for, she got it.

"Fuck All That"

A GREY CATBIRD SOARED OVERHEAD INTO a tree and sat perched in the shade as Perlie walked to work below. He recognized the bird by its call. It was the type that frequently flew over the fortified prison walls—as did robins and crows, and on occasion, a hawk or osprey. He saw buzzards too, but they were hardly worth mentioning. Perlie thought they probably mistook the inmates for decaying animals when they soared over the penitentiary yard.

Perlie was at the garage again, growing more pleased by his freedom each time he entered. He felt the difference in the cadence of his feet. A few repairs were lined up for the morning, all of which could be knocked out easily. But he hadn't counted on the car left out in the front lot of the garage from the night before. The run-down car was already there when he showed up, though he didn't notice it at first. It had clearly been driven hard and left in harm's way a few times before. Perlie spotted a note on the window when he finally went out to investigate. As he got close, he noticed the keys on the seat. A twenty dollar bill sat face up underneath the keys and on the steering wheel was a handwritten note, that said:

GOT A FLAT EARLY
GOT A RIDE 2 WORK
SPARE IN TRUNK
WILL PICK UP AFTER WORK TODAY

Perlie went on working quickly through his other scheduled jobs, making time for the vehicle out front. Later on in the afternoon when he could work on the car with the flat, he jumped in the seat and pulled it around into the garage. Freddie was in his office and had been spending a great deal of time there, either holed up with the door shut or absent from the garage all together. Perlie didn't mind, the jazz playing over the radio always kept him company.

Perlie pulled the handle to open the trunk of the unclaimed car and lifted the carpeted door to pull the spare wheel out. Everything he touched in the trunk was slick with dirt and grease, but the spare wheel appeared to be brand-new and, even more strange, the bolt pattern of the spare didn't match the other wheels on the vehicle. The spare belonged to a different car. Perlie set the wheel down, perplexed and not noticing the money at first. Over the radio, a pair of maracas rattled and an upright bass repeated the same notes loudly. Perlie straightened his back and looked back in the trunk.

In the empty wheel cavity were stacks of banded hundred dollar bills.

"Freddie," Perlie exclaimed. Then, louder, over the radio: "Hey! Freddie."

Freddie arrived at the door quickly. He recognized the alarm in Perlie's face. The beat was really swinging now on the radio, the high toms beating loudly and cymbals crashing violently. Perlie stood in shock with his knees pressed against the open trunk of the filthy car, pointing down into it.

"What is it? What'd you find, Perl? A leg? A arm? What is it?"

"Look," Perlie said, wondering if what he had found was better or worse than an appendage.

That night, a storm blew over Perlie, so incredibly slowly that when the foremost edge of it finally reached the opposite side of town, it rained hard for over an hour. The storm cloud hovered over like a gigantic umbrella—but one in an inverse world like Perlie might have dreamed about, where instead of keeping him dry, thousands of gallons of water dumped from underneath it with the fury of glass marbles. The people of the community hurried home and gathered inside. Birds covered in pairs in canopied trees and beneath the eaves of roofs. Everything and everyone retreated at the noisy onset of the unrelenting rainfall. The sound of the impact was blaring and couldn't be muted by the flailing windshield wipers of motorists that passed by the halfway house.

Perlie fell asleep that evening stuck in a backwards feeling—like the one he knew from incarceration, where time goes on as you sit help-less. There was something about Freddie that Perlie had been afraid to look at head-on, and now he knew it. Perlie recognized the look of merciless destitution that can outweigh reason. He had met a lot of inmates like that.

Now, Perlie lay all the way out into a deep sleep sponsored by the peaceful sound of rain and happy gutters. A vivid dream began again. It had been awhile since he'd had one like it. In the dream, he was anticipating a magician who was trying to pull something from an upside-down derby hat, his finger spinning above it. The magi-cian reached in, grabbing frantically, as if the act had gone horribly wrong. But the flailing was just to distract Perlie from who the magician really was. He recognized the face now—Freddie. After brief trepidation, Perlie focused on the hand again and watched it pull out a stack of bills folded in half. In a flash of lightning the hat became a thunderhead, and then there was a bright flash that jolted Perlie awake.

It was still raining, but more gently. It didn't distract Perlie from the thought of his discovery in the trunk earlier. He lay there with his eyes open—not even trying to sleep, just trying to convince himself to let the whole thing pass until the morning, hoping then that sleep would return. But he couldn't help thinking about the unsettling feeling at the end of the day, the weight he felt in his stomach. That car still hadn't been picked up. There wasn't so much as a phone call asking if it was ready. When Perlie went home, he knew the car wasn't going anywhere. It had been boosted all along.

And he felt the same way about the money that was in the trunk beneath the spare tire—like no one would come for it because the car and the money didn't belong to the person responsible for leaving it behind. They—the car and the money—were surely props abandoned with intent.

Eventually Perlie rose out of bed and got dressed, beckoned by something he couldn't explain. He stopped and thumbed through the brochures that Barb had left him. He found the one for transportation and called a cab to take him to the garage. When the taxi came he crawled out into the storm and the rain.

"Fuck all that," he said, gripping the outside of the cab, slippery in the rain, and lowering himself into it to take him back to the garage.

Perlie returned to the garage in the dark, beckoned by the trunk money or perhaps something else. Not long after he stepped his foot in the door, he heard a car pull up outside the garage. Then heard the key enter the door. It was Freddie, it had to have been—apparently responding to a beckoning of his own. Perlie ducked into the darkness.

Seeming uncertain, Freddie stood in the dark, contemplating. He was really thinking hard about something as Perlie watched him. Suddenly, a second car could be heard arriving. Perlie wondered what was going on. He didn't even see the intruder enter the dark garage.

Neither did Freddie.

Freddie dropped lifeless, like a marionette whose puppeteer unexpectedly lost grip of the control bars. He fell to the garage floor, a heavy heap. There was a quick thud of breath, like the sound that occurs when someone gets clobbered in the gut. Perlie heard it clearly, that final breath, and then thought of Freddie's sudden onset of the irreversible feeling—knowing that life has almost run out. It was the end of life or at least the start of the end that he was witnessing. The moment felt unbearably precise, the duration of it stretched thinly like a drumhead and seemingly lasting longer than the minutes of the day that led to the brutal stabbing.

Perlie wanted to reach out and console Freddie in that final moment as he lay strewn sideways on the polished garage floor. But he couldn't make his presence known to the intruder.

Faint light from the street lamp shone through the door into the front reception but Perlie could hardly make out the intruder in the dark—the one wielding the knife and standing over Freddie.

Now, Perlie was kneeling in a peculiar position against the abandoned car, hunched with one hand firmly on the floor and the fingertips of the other hand barely holding his body, preventing it from falling over. His fingertips were pressed lightly against the quarter panel of the dirty car. *The trap.* Perlie remained still, crouched as he had been when he heard Freddie arrive. He tried to keep his cramped body from quaking.

The intruder waited, watching over Freddie to make sure he was dead. Perlie could see the dark silhouette hovering motionless. Perhaps the intruder knew someone else was in the garage watching. Perlie felt a cold chill cover his arms and his hair stood up straight. The intruder stepped backward through the door into front reception and disappeared behind the wall. Everything was completely still for a moment. The intruder was concealed by the wall of the garage, possibly waiting for Perlie to move or make a sound. Then Perlie heard the flick of a light switch. Light flooded the empty doorway into the garage bay where Freddie laid dead. Nothing moved. Perlie thought it might be a distraction and panicked, quietly looking around the garage bay to make sure he wasn't about to be ambushed. He looked up at the convex mirror in the corner, the one Freddie had used to spot him the day he started at the garage. Perlie couldn't make out anything other than a bright fan of light coming from the doorway. There was nothing else to see—total stillness. He watched the illuminated door again and then saw a shadow cross onto the floor near Freddie's body. In the doorway a slender man emerged slowly. In the reflection, he looked more like a wild animal whose chest rose and fell rapidly as he his breathed heavily.

Finally the man in the doorway switched the light off again and went out the front door in the darkness. Perlie heard the car, with squealing tires, roar off into the night. He cowered, hoping that he would either wake from the terror or dissolve into the night.

When he finally felt justified to move again, Perlie raced to the telephone at the front and dialed the police. Then he returned to the bay, hardly able to see Freddie's body in the dark. Perhaps he was afraid to. He saw the growing pool of dark blood on the polished concrete beneath him. He was dead. Freddie was really dead. Perlie stood in the dark garage not knowing what to do, not believing any of it had been real. He refused to turn on the lights. When the ambulance finally showed up, a paramedic found the switch and flooded the place with fluorescent light.

"Hellfire"

URIELLA THREATENED EXTORTION IF THE money was not returned to her. Through intimidation or exposure, she warned Officer Bledsoe, the man whose name was provided by the informant.

"You took money that was not yours—*my money*—then panicked because of your own guilt. You say you no longer have it and expect me to believe it? How shameful you are, having no problem taking credit for upholding the law, and misleading the people who falsely idolize you, who are led to believe in your ability to protect them. Now, I know who *you* are, Officer Bledsoe. And you will be judged by them—your constituents and peers. And worse, you will be judged by *me*, and I am worse than any judge you might ever encounter. My interpretation of law departs from the traditional, and the punishment will be uncloaking of your veil of virtue. Get me my money back *now*."

Uriella took pride in her ability to speak both eloquently and forcefully, but even she was impressed with her wherewithal in this moment. She would give Officer Bledsoe one day to contact her to give back the money. Bledsoe obliged, fearful for the repercussions she would enforce, the information she had on him—the dirt—she would make public. He suggested that it would require some effort to retrieve the money, but that he could and would have it as soon as possible. Uriella didn't bother wondering where the money was—she knew where it would be, soon enough.

She may have found some irony—humor even—if she had known that the money that she paid Gene to murder Freddie sat only a few feet from his lifeless bleeding body in the garage.

Bledsoe said very little during their phone exchange, taking comfort in now knowing that the stolen money had nothing to do with the state or any integrity test but rather belonged to this woman, Uriella. He knew that he could get it back as easy as he had given it away. And then, he and Blythe would be discharged from the matter. However, his indignation for the tone used by Uriella, a rotten criminal thriving on extortion, provoked mischief of his own in his plan for getting back her money. Coercion—no intimidation, he thought. He would get the money back without a hitch by the same forceful means taught to him by Uriella. It was time to locate the mechanic.

Perlie had begun to notice the sound that nothing makes—that noise, the one that he had heard before but now sounded different inside his own room at the halfway house. It was a constant muted noise—like a rush of air, or the elongated crashing of a single infinite ocean wave. The sound was a gathering of nondescript noises from outside that combined into a nearly inaudible growl.

Over the course of time since his release, Perlie had seen potential in himself—in his position at the garage—only to have it shattered before him as if the opportunity had never existed to begin with. What was next? His vision focused hazily on a spot on the ceiling where the paint brush from the maintenance man had failed to cover the previous coat, before Perlie moved in. The eclipse of his eyelids was the last thing Perlie saw before he was carried away into slumber, the muted silence once again circumambient.

Bledsoe parked and crossed the dark street, carefully, with his weight on his toes, carrying a small plastic gas can. Briefly, a streetlight overhead revealed him with its spotlight until he disappeared into the veil of darkness and mounted the lawn toward the halfway house. He carefully picked out the unit described to him by Blythe as the one which Perlie must have resided in—next to the one on the southwest corner. The units were all dark now, indicating nothing about their inhabitants. This was Bledsoe's last selfish act of desperation, the last part of his plan to frighten the mechanic into quickly giving the money up without hesitation, so that he could pacify Uriella and thereby achieve his own exoneration. This, here and now.

The officer shuffled surreptitiously toward the unit, verified by Blythe as empty and adjacent to the one occupied by Perlie. Fire would provoke the mechanic, no doubt. He needed to be dealt with like the criminal that he was. Uriella said she'd pay the mechanic a visit the next day after he witnessed, firsthand, the destruction that she was capable of. Then he, the ex-convict mechanic, would know the seriousness of the matter as it was imposed to Bledsoe by Uriella. And besides, no one would miss the single halfway house unit, outdated and vacant. Nobody had been living in the one that he was going to burn anyway. Like he'd told himself before, no one would be harmed. In fact, he'd be doing everyone a favor, eliminating one less lousy housing unit that needed maintained.

Criminals don't belong in homes burdened by the public, criminals belong in the penitentiary.

Crouched near the foundation with the cold, still air of the night closing in on his chest, he reached into his pocket and retrieved a book of matches, and set it at his side near the gas can. He combed the area for small sticks and damp leaves. With both hands pressed firmly against the glass, he slid the crawl space window open and built a pile of brush just near edge of the window. He poured gasoline on the ground and all over inside the crawl space. The sound of splashing liquid reverberated, so he steadied the gas tank and let it drain out slow. He scanned the yard one more time and pulled two matches from the book, igniting them. He tossed them into the brush, and then lit two more and threw those into the crawl space beneath the empty unit. It made a loud *fwoosh* sound. Immediately, the bright orange light washed over Officer Bledsoe's face. Crouched in the same posture, he stepped back over the yard between buildings, looking back with despair and watching the fire as it grew. By the time he reached the street he could already hear it roaring on.

Perlie slept soundly, dreaming that he was following Freddie as he walked. He had the same thought that he had in the garage while watching Freddie being stabbed to death—*please let this be a dream.* He ran after Freddie as fast as he could but couldn't catch up. His feet felt heavy in the wet sand below. When Perlie tried to run faster as Freddie evaded him, his shoes stuck to the ground, pulling up sand with each suctioning foothold. He looked down. On his feet were the plastic slip-on sandals issued in the penitentiary. They clopped in the sand like a horse's hooves.

Then Freddie stopped and turned to let Perlie catch up. Perlie tried to see his face—to see if the man he was chasing was who he thought after all. But the face dissolved and vanished entirely. So did the sand. Now, Perlie was standing on smooth bathroom tile cold as stone. When he looked at his feet he recognized the pattern—pale terracotta tile surrounded by stained grout. Freddie was long gone. Perlie was alone now but he felt like he was no longer himself. He no longer recognized his feet. The floor tile was the same as the bathroom in the halfway house. The feeling transcending the dream, comfort flooded Perlie like shimmery velvet until his head became as weightless as a balloon. He fixed his gaze on the bathroom mirror and he knew that he was experiencing a dream again. Perlie looked into the glass and saw his face, appearing younger and softer. His eyes were more devoid of life than he'd ever seen. They flickered from the center of his pupils like a spark seen reflecting on polished gunmetal—that spark slowly grew with intensity, mirroring in each eye identically. Then, spark became fire.

The feeling of warm velour began to wake Perlie's feet.

He awoke to a blazing fire inside his room with raucous popping and crackling. His eyes failed to adjust initially but when they did he saw the wall of bright shapes, hard-edged and blinding, engulfing the wall of his bedroom. Blythe had been mistaken, this unit wasn't empty after all. Perlie sprang from the bed so quickly that his brain hadn't yet told his feet that it was time to go, so when they hit the floor, his knees buckled. Perlie's legs straightened and he heaved his shoulder through the door into the night. Once clear of the heat, he leapt to the ground and gripped his hands tight in the dewy midnight grass. "Hellfire," Perlie muttered.

The roaring flames engulfed the entire unit now. Burning wood popped and crackled. Flaming fireballs dripped slowly at the burning wall near the vinyl windows. Perlie sat on his haunches in the grass and could see into the kitchen as the roof collapsed. Another tenant across the lawn stepped outside then turned back in to phone the police.

Down the block, a car mounted the street with the bright flaming visitation reflecting in its side mirrors. At the wheel was Bledsoe, who turned out into the street and out of sight.

"Are Your Lugs Torqued on Tight?"

"**Y**OU CAN'T EVER TELL WHAT KIND OF trouble one of these men is gonna bring to this place. I personally interview every one of 'em before they move in. Usually they get along just fine. If they don't, they just disappear back into the hands of the law before I even see a sign of trouble. But this? I never expected this, in all my career. I consider this a crime-free zone, really."

Barb adjusted her glasses as she spoke to the investigator.

"That man—when he came to me, he was polite as anyone. Ain't hardly been here but a week. There must've been some reason someone burned his house down with him inside. I never took him for a troublemaker, but I guess he fooled me. Sometimes I think it just follows certain people around."

"What's that?" the investigator asked.

"Pardon?" Barb said looking over the tops of her rims.

"Follows people around?"

"Trouble, I guess. Good lord. He had me fooled."

There was no sound in the garage. No jazz horns or crashing symbols playing over the radio. No whistling in the hall. Not even air hissing from the compressor. Perlie wasn't sure what he was going to do at the garage, but he went in that morning anyway. He just stood there in silence for a moment. He looked down and saw the ground. On the polished concrete was a dark brown stain—a new blemish, one that didn't result from a leaky engine.

The shrill ring of the phone cut through the vacuum of noise, like a razor—startling Perlie so badly he nearly leapt from the ground. Perlie hurried through the doorway to the counter where the phone was and held it to his ear.

"Hello, Autopia," he said, hoping no one was there so he could hang up and think quietly in peace again.

"Who am I speaking to?" a woman's voice asked. "Are you the mechanic?"

"Yeah, this is Perlie."

"This is Uriella. I've seen you before."

He knew who she was. "I see. Well, Freddie's dead. He was killed. You mighta heard."

She responded with a faint, non-committal noise—like a grunt but softer. Her voice had no surprise or sympathy, and she did not even confirm that she understood what he said.

"So … what do you want?" Perlie asked.

"What was your crime?" Uriella asked candidly.

"Pardon?"

"Your crime—that you were sent to the penitentiary for. What was it?"

"I don't—"

"I ask because, as I understand, Freddie had a heart for convicts. For employing them."

"I've heard," Perlie said, saddened at the thought of Freddie, dead.

"Well, you need not say. It doesn't matter, I suppose."

"Okay," Perlie said quietly.

"Do you know the trouble that Freddie found for himself? Did he tell you?" She didn't let Perlie answer. "Of course not, you haven't worked there long enough. His pride, anyhow—"

"No, he didn't say much," Perlie said bitterly. "But he's dead now."

"And?"

"And, so—what's it matter? He's already been freed from … whatever was going on with you two."

"Listen, Perlie—Freddie owed me a great deal. He *still* owes me, but I've arranged for eventual full repayment. Freddie borrowed from a lot of people. He sealed his own fate."

"I see," Perlie said, softly. He wished he hadn't answered the phone and gotten himself involved, more than he already was.

Uriella sighed into the phone heavily. "Unsurprisingly, he took money that did not belong to him recently. Did you know about this?"

Perlie thought about the cash in the trunk.

Uriella went on. "Either way. Maybe that doesn't matter. I don't wish to get more parties involved. Freddie took some money. Perhaps he was going to use it to begin to settle his debt with me. I doubt it." She paused. "An indebted man like Freddie, suddenly awarded cash, well … he doesn't use it to make payments on debt. He spends it, the same way he did when he got into debt in the first place. I guess, what I'm hoping is that he didn't have time to do so. Maybe it's still there, at Autopia. Did you ever see him hide anything? Anything recently?"

"I don't know. I … maybe. I can think—"

"Of course you can. Well, I had an idea—just now. And, you don't need to incriminate yourself. I'll wait while you go take a look and see what you can find." She spoke pragmatically.

"Yeah, I can do that. Hang on a minute." Perlie set the phone down on the counter. He went to the deserted car beside the discolored floor. Perlie looked at the spot where the tips of his fingers held him still on the side of the car the night before, opposite the blood stain. He looked at the distance in the daylight, realizing just how close he had been to Freddie and the intruder. Quickly, he cleaned his prints from the dusty car and lifted the trunk open. He returned and picked up the phone.

"I've got it," Perlie said. He decided Uriella would appreciate how quickly he found the money and thought it was best not to explain how he knew where it could be found.

"You did well. Now, I just need a favor. You see, I'm up the coast on some business. I've stopped at a payphone but I'd like to meet you near Rockport Beach this afternoon. Can you do that?"

Perlie agreed. He relaxed, knowing she wouldn't come anywhere near the garage, not now, right after Freddie's murder.

Upon checkout at a pump station near the coast Perlie found himself having a conversation with the clerk after driving in silence for some time. Their chat was chummy and for that Perlie was pleased. It was the casual conversations—the innocent ones—that Perlie enjoyed, like the type he might have had with Deuce, or with Freddie at the garage. He thought of Freddie—of the tune that he whistled relentlessly that day. He missed the banter between two working men—like he once had with Chambers, too, back when he was delivering produce, before he sold Perlie out to the cops to save his own ass. Now the conversation was with an attendant and Perlie felt like a man who had just left the last shift he'd ever work at Freddie's garage.

The attendant asked, "Headin' far today?" He looked through Perlie, his gaze fixed on the built-in cooler on the back wall.

"Hope not," Perlie responded, standing on the opposite side of the counter.

The attendant took Perlie's money and looked down at the register, hitting the keys furiously until the drawer ejected.

"Well, no matter either way, but if you're headed north on County 33 ..." The attendant paused to gather the change from the drawer. "You are headed north, right?" His eyes shifted to Perlie's worn out truck, the one Freddie used to drive, faded green with rust on the wheel wells. It sat outside the filling station in the gravel drive. The attendant looked at the truck, its front bumper pointed north as the midday sun left waves of heat broiling from the decaying paint.

"Yeah, yeah. You're right," Perlie said.

"Well—if you're headed north on 33," the attendant said, his extended fingers fluttering northward, "eventually ... well, you're in for a real treat."

"Why is that?" Perlie asked, concerned.

"Only kidding, 'course. Because the road just north a here is a mangled mess for about two to three ... or four miles, straight through. Whole damn way. I always try to warn people headed north. People I don't know. And I ... don't know you." The attendant smiled.

"Got it," Perlie said. "Thanks for the tip. I'll keep my eye out."

"Yeah ... the county roads seldom get any attention from the road crew. They haven't been repaved in who knows how long." He looked up, thinking. "Probably five years. I've been working here for over four and I've never even seen so much as one road cone on it. I drive home that way every night—I live up there in the canyon, so I haven't got a choice, see? If that stretch could be avoided easily, I'd do it. But it's just not an option. Unless you drive a dune buggy, maybe."

The door swung open and a customer walked in. The cashier looked over briefly and greeted him casually. The man waved back nonchalantly.

"Great hounds of hell," the attendant went on, "those roads are rough. Be careful—don't want you snapping an axle or something. How are your wheels? Are your lugs torqued on tight?"

Perlie looked out the window and said, "I think it's all taken care of. I'll be careful."

Hawks floated and swirled in the wind above the

trees. At least they looked like hawks to Perlie, but he couldn't tell for sure, as they were silhouetted against the sky. He was enjoying driving and seeing the landscape outside of town for the first time since his release. Trees were perched like ancient gods among the faint ocean spray that diffused along the shore, arriving from the middle of the sea. A putrid odor of decayed wood and wet sand dissipated in the steady flow of air inside the cab. The sky was grey like worn concrete. Clouds were almost indiscernible and raced at varying speeds above the car, dropping mist on the windshield like a saturated shower mirror.

The motor of the work truck buzzed, muffled by fierce wind, on a road twisted and uneven. The past that sat behind Perlie was abandoned and he moved ahead with eyes forward. The ridge rose gradually, and with it his spirit. Perlie's unimpeded view was like a lighthouse with a seized cog, no longer spinning and aimed fixed where the sea and coast wed before him. Perlie could no longer handle the silence and so he flicked on the radio, the dial already set to the jazz station that Freddie adored. A song had just began, the piano keys twinkling, searching for the rhythm while the saxophone played in long sorrowful notes, guiding the melody along. Suddenly the tempo locked in, the low horns repeated steadily, and after a few bars came the flute on top, wheezing and sparkling.

Perlie recognized the tune—Freddie's whistling that day. Here it was, the real thing. A quick build-up—a rapid progression, followed by several long notes, drawn out and tired. Over and over again. He wished it would go on forever.

Perlie met Uriella in a parking lot used by beach-goers, dotted with curbed gardens and flanked on either side by great palms with their trunks tightly wrapped, their fronds fanning in the breeze. The pavement was wet—not from rain but from saturated sea air.

There she stood, looking out over the ocean: Uriella. She wore a red dress and thick black sunglasses, which Perlie recognized from the first day he had seen her outside of the garage. She turned and looked at Perlie in the work truck as he pulled in. Her arms were crossed and her dark hair blew wildly around her head. Perlie parked next to where she stood and killed the engine.

She had to shout over the howling wind. "You carrying a weapon?"

"Nope. No weapon. You?" Perlie climbed out of the car.

She ignored his question. "You have the cash?"

"Yeah." He handed her the deposit bag that contained the money he and Freddie found in the trunk.

"Are you carrying a weapon?" Perlie asked again. The wind blew fiercely.

Uriella walked to the driver's side door of her gleaming coupe and entered. She left the door open with one leg hanging out above the asphalt parking lot. "Of course," she finally responded. "I always am."

She reached into the deposit bag and counted the bills. She paused counting for a moment and locked the passenger door, near where Perlie was standing. Then she pushed a button that opened the glove box. Inside, Perlie saw a large revolver and a box of ammunition. Uriella looked at Perlie through her sunglasses and then cranked her passenger window down no more than an inch.

"All I can say is that I'm sorry that you have lost your friend," she said from inside the coupe. "Truly, it is a shame, for your sake. But a man like him cannot be stopped. The fate of anyone cannot be … reconciled. Especially for a man like Freddie."

She counted some more and then continued. "Freddie thought highly of money … and gambling. He put it all above everything else and couldn't be convinced otherwise. Some people will do anything for money. Even kill." She finished counting and bounced the bills straight like a deck of cards. Then she re-banded them tightly and closed the bag, placing it in the glovebox with her revolver. She pushed the glovebox closed. "It's all here. Looks like none of it was gambled away after all. Who knows what he would have done if he had more time."

Uriella lifted her leg into the car and pulled the door shut.

Perlie heard the motor start. "We finished, you and me?" he asked. "I don't gotta worry about you?"

"Freddie's death was all business," she said. "It had nothing to do with you."

"What about my house?"

"What about it?"

"Somebody burned it down last night. I was sleeping inside. I could've been killed."

If she was shocked, Perlie couldn't tell through her dark sunglasses. Uriella sat still a moment and then her head bobbed delicately. "Bledsoe ... cops."

Perlie heard her but didn't understand. Then Uriella said, "You have my word that this is over between you and I. Now you can go on living your life. However, there is something else..."

"A Time for Everything"

THE MOTOR HUMMED ALONG IN THE WORK truck, the black asphalt road spooling beneath the wheels. Perlie thought of the utter calamity since his release from the penitentiary. He almost wanted to go back just to get away from it.

Onward he drove down the same crippled County 33 toward home, this time the sea on the opposite side of the car. It made the drive back feel different.

Now he headed back to watch Freddie be lowered into the ground, where he would be kept in his place. Either in the grave or back behind bars—that's where Uriella thought Freddie would have wound up eventually. The righteous must be able to locate the eternally damned—the ones incapable of change. The virtuous stood dignified aboveground. At the end of the day, Freddie was a sinner. Through his death came the necessary placement of a counterweight, or maybe it was the removal of one. Perlie wondered if it was better to be dead or to be damned.

He rolled along closer to the city. A row of wild flowers bordered the road, flowers that appeared indigenous only to heaven, they sprawled among smooth and infinite pebbles that led to the sea and then up the base of the mountains, covering the ground where the yarrow and primrose grew.

Perlie pulled up to the graveyard and drove along the wrought-iron fence that surrounded broken headstones that looked like a mess of slanted teeth. Circled around a freshly dug hole in the ground were a few of Freddie's loved ones. He recognized Will, the man who came in the shop that day, filled with laughter and speaking about the races. Perlie wondered how everyone else there knew Freddie. He wondered how they would remember Freddie. For what kinds of things? Perlie debated if the sins of someone's life were forgiven upon death and only then. Who would forgive someone like Freddie? Or like Deuce? Like Perlie? Perlie remembered hearing once, *God doesn't rescue the damned from their fallen condition*.

At the cemetery, the people waited for the priest as they gathered close. Perlie got out of the truck and heard someone say that they'd just come from the clergy house and that the priest was going to be late.

Perlie ceased walking. He didn't want to wait and didn't feel like talking. He'd just come back after a while. He turned and got back in the truck. Freddie's mother recognized his son's old work truck as it drove back out through the cemetery gates.

Earlier, it was Uriella who said to Perlie, "I cannot do anything for you. Nor do I feel as though I should. As I've said, nothing could be done for your friend. Even men of principle are subject to greed. That cost him his life, you see. But you must understand there is nothing that could happen naturally to expel that greed or to rectify it. It had to be stopped cold in its tracks. By me. But maybe there is something now that could be done. However, it comes with risk … risk that I don't need. Risk that I won't take. I do not wish to meddle in the affairs of those cops or agents any longer. Their *tests*. That is no longer my business and I wish to put the whole ordeal behind me. But I did think, *for you* … if you wish to balance things out. For the balance of justice, or injustice rather. For efficacy. There is something that could be done, Mr. Perlie—the mechanic..

"There is another bundle of money at the apartment of someone I know. 4000 Simshaw. That money does not belong to me. It does not belong to anyone, really. The cops were supposed to take it but took mine instead. They took the wrong money, the wrong bait. Never mind that … how ignorant of all parties. Perhaps their god is holding out for a better moment to make an example of us all."

…doesn't rescue the damned…

"But I believe that *that* bundle of money remains beneath the mattress, in the bedroom. It will stay there until some other crooked cops are called there. Then they will get caught like the other two were supposed to. Don't you see? They left it—the bait, the *integrity test*—for some other cretin. All they have to do is call in the address when they're ready to make an example of some crooked cops. Maybe even the same cops. I should hope not, though. But unchecked greed only emboldens them, I've learned.

"But you, Perlie, *you* have no connection, officially. And now the money just sits there, waiting to be taken. And to whom does it belong? To who *should* it belong? That is not for me to say, but I've heard it said that money only belongs to the one who holds it. So, if you wish, hold it. Take it. Then all that will remain will be the blame. But not *your* blame.

"Take it," Uriella softly said.

Perlie drove from the cemetery and arrived at the address, pulling the work truck to the side of the street about a half block from the address on Simshaw Avenue. He sat briefly, watching. He'd have to move quickly if he wanted to get back to the graveyard before the priest started the service. Something cut through Perlie, piercing like a knife blade. Fear had followed him everywhere but now it was gone. He'd arrived at Simshaw Avenue feeling more cruel than before.

Carefully but deliberately, Perlie opened the door to 4000 Simshaw Avenue.

The pastor had arrived and was already speaking from his pulpit of vivid green artificial turf. A few people stood around the hole, sorrowfully, with their heads bowed, standing tucked between battered headstones. The pastor rushed into the service, feeling awful for his delayed arrival. He spoke with pride.

"There is a time for everything and a season for every activity under the heavens," said the pastor. "A time to be born and a time to die ..."

"... a time to plant and a time to uproot ..."

"... a time to tear down and a time to build ..."

Perlie made his way into the bedroom at 4000 Simshaw blindly, his vision shock stricken and tunneled. He moved his rubbery legs. His feet felt like chintzy slippers in heavy sand. Then he was weightless, the power he held over himself was fleeting, and he was driven forward irrevocably. In the bedroom he pried the mattress up, revealing the bounty. The integrity test.

Perlie stuffed the bills into his pockets violently and when he clutched every last bill he dropped the mattress down, expelling a whiff of dust and blight into the warm air.

Outside the bedroom, there was a noise, the thud of a car door as Perlie passed back through the bedroom door to the foyer. Someone was outside. Petrified, his blood became cold and thick.

Freddie's mother began to weep softly from a folding chair in the graveyard. She had lost her son—the only one given to her by God. Freddie, a man of two worlds who had now left them both. She knew her son had faults, but she considered him a man of character. Freddie, stuck with a knife and slaughtered in cold blood. She felt indignation for his untimely death. Freddie's mother wondered if her boy had made it to heaven. Afflicted with grief at the thought of the other place where condemned souls gather, she began to howl.